CHRISTMAS WISHES FOR THE BLETCHLEY PARK GIRLS

THE LILY BAKER SERIES BOOK 6

PATRICIA MCBRIDE

Boldwood

First published in 2022. This edition first published in Great Britain in 2024 by Boldwood Books Ltd.

Copyright © Patricia McBride, 2022

Cover Design by Colin Thomas

Cover Photography: Colin Thomas, Alamy and Unsplash

The moral right of Patricia McBride to be identified as the author of this work has been asserted in accordance with the Copyright, Designs and Patents Act 1988.

Every effort has been made to obtain the necessary permissions with reference to copyright material, both illustrative and quoted. We apologise for any omissions in this respect and will be pleased to make the appropriate acknowledgements in any future edition.

A CIP catalogue record for this book is available from the British Library.

Paperback ISBN 978-1-83561-043-5

Large Print ISBN 978-1-83561-044-2

Hardback ISBN 978-1-83561-042-8

Ebook ISBN 978-1-83561-045-9

Kindle ISBN 978-1-83561-046-6

Audio CD ISBN 978-1-83533-997-8

MP3 CD ISBN 978-1-83533-998-5

Digital audio download ISBN 978-1-83561-041-1

Boldwood Books Ltd
23 Bowerdean Street
London SW6 3TN
www.boldwoodbooks.com

1

OCTOBER 1942

'How long have you and been courting now?' Bronwyn asked as we walked towards the fish and chip shop.

I counted the weeks. 'Nearly three months. Not that we see each other often, with shift work and him being away so much.'

'Almost as long as it took him to pluck up courage to ask you out then!' Bronwyn said with a cheeky grin. 'I thought he'd never get round to it.'

'Nor did I, but it was worth the wait. And I reckon it's going to be a good month for the country. Three German U-boats sunk already!'

'One Japanese one, and all,' Bronwyn added. 'I wonder if the war will end soon. It'd be wonderful if it would.'

Fallen leaves in their fine gold, red and brown covered the footpath like an elaborate carpet brightening up the otherwise dull day. A brown and white dog walked up to us and pushed his nose against my leg. Absentmindedly, I scratched behind its ear then wondered if it had fleas.

A minute later we shooed it away and went into the chip

shop, glad fish and chips weren't rationed. The smell of frying batter and malt vinegar drew us in like children following the Pied Piper. Of course we had to queue, but enjoyed listening to the Bletchley Town gossip.

The walls were a dull cream, and although it was clean, there was always a sheen of grease on the walls. There were several war posters on display. My favourite showed three women in their pinnies, one holding a banner declaring 'Up housewives and at 'em! Put out your metal, paper, bones!'

I looked at the menu on the wall, not that there was much choice. Chips were a penny and fish tuppence. As I was getting threepence ready, a chauffeur in an immaculate posh uniform came in and stood behind us.

'Come to collect plaice and chips for Colonel and Mrs Smythers,' he said as if we'd asked. 'They'll have to pay sixpence for their fish. Plaice they have. They're too grand for cod. Daft sods. I can't tell the difference.'

Neither could I, not that I remembered ever having plaice – at home we always thought that was for people who were above us.

We walked down the road eating our fish and chips out of newspaper. It was a gusty October day and several times I had to grab hold of my food as the wind caught the edges of the paper. The hardware shop we passed had its usual display of saucepans and other household objects. Not as many as there used to be, and I wondered if that was because the government needed all the metals it could get for weapons.

Bronwyn saw me looking. 'Good job Happy Days has got a brick wall round the front garden. If it'd had railings they'd be long gone.'

Happy Days was the former bed and breakfast run by our landlady, Mrs. W. There were four of us girls from Bletchley Park there. Me and Bronwyn, Peggy and Carolyn. Peggy was one of the barmaids in the Beer Hut at the Park, as we called it, and a real live wire. I didn't know what Carolyn did. During our interviews it had been drilled into us never to talk about our work – 'Careless talk costs lives' and all that. Me and Bronwyn both spent our working days decoding messages from France. We often didn't understand the significance of them, or even know who they came from. Sometimes we didn't understand the French because the words were unfamiliar, and sometimes the reception was so bad we missed half the message. But we were assured it was vital work for the war effort, to help us beat the awful Nazis. We knew better than to ask questions.

'Come on, it's not too cold yet. Let's take a turn round the park before we head back home,' Bronwyn said. 'I needs to stretch my legs after sitting with headphones on for hours.'

It was late afternoon, and the light was beginning to fade. As we walked, a flock of migrating birds flew overhead in perfect formation and we could faintly hear the beating of their wings. The air had that sort of crisp, clean autumn feel, disturbed only by the smell of a very distant bonfire. Two boys, their bare knees scabbed, were sailing a toy boat on the lake, shouting encouragement to it as if it could hear them.

We strolled, breaking off pieces of fish and chips to eat with our fingers as we chatted.

'You haven't had a boyfriend for ages,' I said to Bronwyn. 'Or if you have you've kept quiet about them.'

She threw a chip at me. It missed. 'Not being funny or nothing, but you're as subtle as a ton of bricks. I told you, I gave up married men ages ago. And let's face it, there's not a lot of men to choose from up at the Park.'

'There's a few,' I said. 'That's where I met Grant, after all.'

She screwed her newspaper up tight and wiped her greasy fingers on her hankie. 'Let's face it, most of them are married or wouldn't know a woman if one bit them in the neck.' She paused. 'But there's one...'

I stopped walking and turned to face her. 'You've met someone?'

The boys whose boat had gone a little out of reach interrupted us. They were panicking, and about to go into the water.

'STOP!' Bronwyn shouted, grabbing one of them by the collar. 'You don't know how deep that water is.'

'But my boat...' he said, his face as tragic as if his mother had died.

She let him go and looked around. 'Go and grab that long bit of branch over there. We'll see if we can hook it back.'

'Coo, that's clever,' the other boy said, scratching his almost shaven head hard enough to make me wonder if he had nits like the dog.

We had to walk a little way round the lake to get closer to the boat, but Bronwyn hooked it first try. 'There, boyo, now you'll know what to do if it happens again, won't you.'

The boy looked at her. 'You talk funny,' he said.

'Don't be so cheeky,' she said, pretending to clip him round the ear. 'I talks like this because I'm not English. Where do you think I come from?'

The boy frowned and thought for a minute. 'Africa? You've got curly hair like someone in a book at school.'

She laughed. 'No, silly boy. I'm from Wales.'

The other boy spoke up. 'Where's that then? Is it in America?'

She tousled his hair. 'Look it up on an atlas at school or ask any grown up. They'll know.' She took a proper look at their toy boat. 'That's a nice boat. Where did you get it from? There's not many toys in the shops these days.'

The second boy spoke up. 'The German prisoners of war made them for us.'

I'd heard the prisoners were building an estate on what had been a playing field. 'So you go and talk to them?' I asked.

'Yeah. They're nice. They like talking to us. Can't understand most of 'em 'cos they talk funny, too.'

The church bell struck and he jumped. 'Crikey, come on, mate. We'd better get going.' And with that, they ran across the park without another word.

I suddenly remembered what we'd been talking about and grabbed Bronwyn's arm.

'So have you? Met someone?'

She wrapped her coat tighter round her and gave a wry smile. 'Not as such. But there's a bloke I chat to sometimes in the canteen.' She carried on walking.

'So?' I said, desperate to know more.

She raised an eyebrow. 'So nothing. We just chat sometimes. Nothing more. He's a widower with a young daughter.'

I thought about what I knew of her home life in Swansea. She'd often talked about her younger siblings. She regularly moaned about them, but always in a fond way.

The temperature was dropping and we walked faster towards home, kicking up the leaves like a couple of kids.

We opened the front door and immediately knew Mrs. W was in. She and Donnie, her husband, lived in an annex attached to the main house but she was always in and out keeping an eye on things. The smell of cigarette smoke was a dead giveaway she was there somewhere. As we took our coats off, clattering from the kitchen told us where she was.

'Hello, ducks!' she said, the fag hanging out of one corner of her mouth making her squint. 'I was sorting things out for you. Fancy a cuppa?'

Without waiting for an answer, she put the kettle on. 'We're halfway through October already. You girls got anything planned for Halloween?'

I got out the cups and saucers. 'We've changed our shifts so we can help with the school Halloween party. Should be fun. The poor kids don't get much of that with the war on.'

Mrs. W. took the big brown teapot off the shelf. 'I heard they're so short of paper down at the school that the kids have to write in pencil in their exercise books. Then when they're full, they start again and write in pen over the top. What's the world coming to when they have to do that?'

The kettle whistled and we made the tea, then we sat round the well-scrubbed table. Mrs. W. got a little flask out of her bag and tipped some of the contents into her tea. It was clear, so probably vodka. It was surprising she didn't go up in flames with the spirits and the smoking.

'I know you girls can't talk about your work. Come to that, I don't even know what your work is...' she started.

'We've told you. We're just typists. Boring work,' Bronwyn said. Everyone got the same story.

'Well,' Mrs. W. went on. 'I've been hearing the most dreadful rumours about what them Nazis are up to. Killing thousands of Jews, just for being Jewish. If that's true, they must be the worst people on this earth.'

Although people didn't talk about their work at the Park, we had begun to hear terrible stories about Auschwitz, but we couldn't say. 'Where did you hear that?' I asked.

She knocked her cigarette ash into her saucer. 'Mr Hoffman at the butcher's shop told me. He said he got a letter from his cousin in Germany saying they had to get out of the country quick. He was worried they'd left it too late.'

'Let's hope it's not. No wonder he's worried if those rumours are true. We think we're hard done by with this war dragging on. They're putting up with a lot worse.'

Mrs. W.'s lips pursed. 'I meant to talk to you girls about that. Now that soap's rationed, you've got to be a lot more careful. More than once I've found the soap left in the water. It'll be gone in no time if you do that.'

We apologised, but knew the culprit was Carolyn who never quite got the idea of having to be careful about anything you could buy.

As we spoke, we heard footsteps on the stairs. Carolyn came into the kitchen wearing her uniform. 'Right, ladies. I'm off to work. See you in the morning.'

Mrs. W. watched her go. 'I don't know how you girls do it. And what sort of letters are so important that you have to type them at night. That's what I don't understand.' She flicked the ash from her cigarette into her saucer. 'Me, I'd fall asleep by midnight, sure as eggs is eggs.'

* * *

If Bronwyn and I had ordered the weather for Halloween, we couldn't have done better than nature provided. It was a dull, dreary day with low menacing clouds that threatened rain any minute. Smoke from coal fires in every house added to the gloom. Even at midday, we could imagine witches flying out of those clouds to terrorise little ones.

'Gotta say, girl,' Bronwyn said with a smile. 'It won't be hard to get the little blighters in the mood today. Lush, it is. Perfect for giving them the heebie-jeebies.'

We were walking to the school hall where the Halloween party was to take place after classes had ended. Teachers had already had fun with them, making masks and colouring pumpkin-shaped cardboard.

'Is your Grant still on to do some magic tricks?' Bronwyn asked as we entered the school playground. Some girls were skipping to a rhyme I hadn't heard before:

> *This little pig went to Brighton*
> *Another little pig went too*
> *The first little pig dropped a bomb on the town*
> *And the second dropped another, then flew*
> *But both little pigs were shot out of the air*
> *And fell in the ocean blue*

'Great rhyme,' I said, 'but what a pity they grow up knowing about such things. Thank goodness we don't get bombed round here.'

Bronwyn lowered her voice. 'If the Nazis knew what we are up to in Bletchley Park, we'd be bombed in a heartbeat. But you didn't answer about Grant.'

'Barring emergencies, he'll be here. I hope you aren't expecting great things. He's no magician. He's just learned some simple tricks he hopes the kids won't see through.'

I'd watched him practise the previous day in our break from work. We usually spent any snatched time together with nothing more on our minds than ourselves. This day, however, we were on a mission.

We'd found an empty office and Grant produced his magic equipment with a flourish, summoning Abracadabra! with a grin. After a hesitant start, he managed to find a coin behind my ear, then he had three card tricks, and a trick where the kids try to stir pepper in a glass. Only he would be able to do it.

'Has he got a big finale trick?' Bronwyn asked.

I smiled. 'He wouldn't tell me what it was, but he said it'll end with a bang. The whole lot won't take more than fifteen minutes. He's dead worried it'll go wrong.'

'No need to worry about that. The kids'll love it if it does. They like nothing better than showing adults up.'

Working with three mothers, we used the masks and coloured-in pumpkins to decorate the hall. One of the mothers, Enid, had an artistic eye and guided the rest of us in our endeavours.

'Right,' she said when we'd finished. 'We've decided our games. Who's going to get them going? We'll all be needed to keep them under control.' Before we knew it, she had us all given roles, and said she would make sure everything happened as planned. We believed her.

Grant arrived ten minutes before the party was due to start. He set up a table, with his equipment and then covered it with a piece of fabric black as night. 'I'm going to wait elsewhere,' he said. 'I've got to maintain an air of mystery and I could do with a cuppa if I'm honest.' He looked at me. 'Can you spare a minute?'

I followed him into the hall, nervous at the seriousness in his voice.

'Lily, I'm afraid I've got to go away for a week. I'll be leaving immediately I finish here.'

My heart sank. Even though we didn't see each other for days on end sometimes, I liked to feel he wasn't far away. The fact that we both worked at the Park meant we could feel close even if our shifts didn't overlap. We didn't even work in the same buildings. He was in the big house and me and Bronwyn were in one of the wooden huts.

I wanted to ask where he was going, but knew he wouldn't be able to tell me. We were all so used to keeping everything secret at the Park that I'd grown as skilled at deception as a magician myself.

Falling into his arms, I kissed him briefly on the lips. 'Keep safe, my love.'

If only I'd had any idea what would happen to him.

No sooner had I got back into the hall than the children began to arrive. Life had been very boring for most of them with the restrictions of war. Rationing, restricted travel, fathers away, and worry about bombing all meant they were ready for fun. We were determined to give them some.

'Best to start with a game to burn off some steam first,' wise Enid had said. With that in mind, we had them searching for hidden vampire bats. They were small, made of black card and hidden about the hall. They'd found them all in less than ten minutes.

Next they played pass the parcel, where the prize was a small bar of dark chocolate. Then tin can bowling. We'd painted some empty tins with silly, scary faces and they had to try to knock them down with small bean bags. Two other games, then it was time for tea.

Many of the children were from poor families, so the idea of extra food was exhilarating. The bigger ones helped us set up the tables, drag the chairs in place and fetch the food from the kitchen. It was a modest feast – fish paste sandwiches, Spam and Marmite, and cheese and carrot. Nothing fancy but they were gone in a flash and it was the quietest they'd been since they came into the hall. The sandwiches were followed by rock cakes and jam tarts.

Enid organised them to help clear up, then it was time for Grant. Enid nudged me. 'Go on, Lily, introduce him so the kids think he's a big deal performer.'

I stepped onto the stage and held up my hand. 'Okay, everyone, I want you to be on your best behaviour because we have someone very special now. A world-famous magician who is going to amaze you with his magic tricks.' I pretended to do a drum roll. 'May I introduce the Magic Magician, the great Caraveno!' I knew he was waiting in the wings, so I held out my arm and he walked on. He not only had his cape, but also a top hat which he twirled with a flourish.

'Ladies and gentlemen, boys and girls,' he said in some strange accent I couldn't place. 'I am the famous Caraveno and you will be amazed, staggered, awestruck at what you are about to see.'

He went down the three steps from the stage to the children and with many a twirl of his cape, he found pennies behind the ears of four children. They gasped and rubbed where the pennies were supposed to have been, hoping to find more.

'Got one for me, Mister?' a boy shouted.

'Who is brave enough to speak to the Great Caraveno?' he asked, looking around.

A tiny lad with hair so short it looked shaven, put up both hands. 'It was me. Can I 'ave a penny too, Mister?'

Grant wagged a finger to call him over. 'Now, you, sir, if you help me with my next trick, I may be able to find a penny behind your ear, too.'

'Cor, are you for real?' the lad said, hitching up his socks which had fallen round his ankles.

Suppressing a smile, Grant asked him to come up on stage. 'What's your name?' he whispered.

'Jonno,' the boy replied, turning pink.

Grant turned to the audience again. 'Right, everyone, give this brave young man, Jonno, a big round of applause. He has no idea if he'll survive being up here with me. I might even cut him in half!'

Jonno went pale. 'You won't, will you, Mister?' he pleaded.

Grant replied by winking at him.

With many more flourishes, swishes and cries of 'Abra-cadabra!' Grant did three card tricks with Jonno. He managed to make each of them last much longer than when we'd practised. At the end of the third one, he bowed low to the boy and turned to the audience. 'Now, ladies and gentlemen, before this brave young man returns to his seat, I think he deserves a round of applause.'

As he performed, I enjoyed watching the faces of the children in the audience. They were wide eyed watching the simple tricks, whispering to each other excitedly. But my thoughts turned to Grant's news that he was going away. Would he be going some-where safe? If he went to their office in London, he could be in danger of being bombed. My time as an Air Raid Precautions worker meant I had plenty of first-hand knowledge of what bombs could do to a body. A man I loved deeply had died in one such raid. It had taken a long time for me to recover from that loss.

Jonno's voice brought me round from my reverie. 'Wot about my penny, Mister?' Jonno asked when the applause died down. His mouth was turned down at the corners. 'Did you forget, Mister?'

Grant twirled his cape again. 'I, the great Caraveno, never forget. But you have to do one more thing for me before you get your reward.' He produced a spoon from a pocket in his cloak and handed it to the lad.

'Now, you're a strong lad. I wonder if you can you bend that spoon before I count to twenty?' As he counted, Jonno struggled to bend the spoon, going redder in the face as the numbers got higher.

At twenty, Grant stopped him. 'You've done very well, young man. But it was a very strong spoon and can only be bent by the Great Caraveno. No one else in this room would be able to bend it. Only I, the Great Caraveno!' Grunting and pretending to struggle, he bent it, then waved it about for everyone to see. There were loud gasps from the children. I overheard one girl saying, 'I'm going to do that when I get home.'

'Now, my lad. Jonno, the brave one, the Great Caraveno must find your reward!' With a quick movement, Grant put his hand behind Jonno's ear and produced a sixpence. Jonno's mouth dropped open. It was probably more than he'd ever had before. 'Cor, is that all for me?'

'It is, because you're a brave young man. Now you can sit down again. Thank you for your help.' He paused and turned to the audience again. 'Another round of applause for our brave volunteer!'

His final trick was to pull a string of silk fabric hankies out of his top hat, making them float in the air.

I stepped on stage again when he'd finished. 'That was amazing. Come on, kids, let's give the great Caraveno a big round of applause!'

I stood on tiptoe and kissed him on the cheek. It got more laughs and applause than all the tricks put together.

Bronwyn had been helping to keep the kids in order and generally organising. As the parents came to collect them, she spotted Thomas, the man she spoke to in the canteen queue.

'I didn't know you'd be here today,' he said when he spotted her.

Before she could answer a little girl ran up and threw herself at him. 'This is my daughter, Bella,' he said by way of introduction.

Bella ignored Bronwyn and pulled at her father's arm. 'I'll see you again,' he called as he left the hall.

'That your bloke?' I asked, having seen what happened. 'He's got a kind face.'

Bronwyn put her hands on her hips. 'I gotta say, Lily, you gotta get it in your head, he's not my bloke. I just talks to him like, sometimes.'

But I had seen that look on her face before and didn't believe a word of it.

2

I pulled my headset off, feeling frazzled after concentrating for hours as I listened to messages from France. Although I often only heard fragments or couldn't understand the importance of what I was hearing, sometimes I understood more than I wished to. Numbers of dead, resistance fighters captured, failure to blow up a bridge important to the German advance, shortage of ammunition. All these and more were part of my everyday work and sometimes I wanted to put my head in my hands and weep at what I made out.

Bronwyn and I were on the same shift that day and finished at the same time. This was my favourite shift, from 8 a.m. to 4 p.m. I loved getting a decent night's sleep, yet having a lot of the day free from four o'clock.

'Come on, my beaut, I'm done in,' Bronwyn said as we put on our coats. 'How about going to see Peggy in the Beer Hut before we head for home?'

A lager sounded exactly the ticket, but I wanted to clear my head of all the sad things I'd heard first. 'Let's walk around the lake, take the long way, then I'll be ready for a drink.'

'A ling de long, is it?' she replied.

I glanced at her as if she'd gone mad. 'What on earth does "ling de long" mean? Is it French?'

She laughed and put her arm through mine. 'No, silly, it's Welsh. It's means a stroll, like what we're doing. Going nowhere in particular.'

I thought I knew all Bronwyn's Welsh expressions, but that was a new one on me. 'Come on then, let's ling de long quicker before we get too cold. Hey, did you hear Clark Gable got made second lieutenant, so he can have a moustache again.'

'I'd have him with or without that moustache,' she replied with a grin.

It was dusk, and the air was still and crisp. Later, there would be millions of stars and a clear moon. A bomber's moon, we called it. As we strolled, the scent of nearby pine trees and, faintly, smoke from the nearest houses reached us. As we circled the pond, there was an occasional splash, but in the gloom we couldn't tell what was moving on the water. Bats flew overhead, and an owl hooted, making me jump.

Although we'd been at Bletchley Park for a while, we didn't know what happened in the other huts we passed every day. We noticed people going in and out of them, but they carried nothing that would give away their work. The only sounds from the huts were of chairs being pushed back, phones ringing, and sometimes a voice raised. Never raised enough for us to make out what was being said, though. In the big house we heard machinery, but had no idea what it was or what it did.

'Did you notice they're getting ready to put up another hut?' Bronwyn asked, guiding me past a tree I was about to walk into. 'I've lost count of how many we have. I wonder how many people work here now. If the queues in the canteen get any longer, we'll never have time to eat.'

'Not that we'll be missing much.'

She nudged me. 'Stop your chompsing, girl. At least we haven't had to cook it or use our rations. Be grateful for tasteless mercies, that's what I say.'

The one hut you always heard noise from was the Beer Hut. The smell of beer and cigarette smoke guided us in, and we headed straight to the bar to see Peggy.

"Ello, girls,' she said with a smile, getting our glasses ready. 'Usual, is it? 'Arf of Shandy, or are you going to push the boat out and 'ave a pint?'

She poured our drinks, then had to serve a couple of other people before she had time to chat.

'Guess what! I just 'eard, I'm going to be an aunt. My sister, Marion, is 'aving a nipper.'

'Aren't you already an aunt?' I asked, then wished I'd bitten my tongue. Peggy had a secret. She'd got in the family way, and her boyfriend had done the dirty on her. Marion had taken baby Linda in, and everyone believed she was her own child. So Linda was growing up believing Peggy was her aunt.

I slapped my hand over my mouth. 'Oh, I'm so...'

'Don't worry about it, sweet'eart,' she said. 'No 'arm done. The new one'll be company for little Linda, so I'm chuffed about that.'

With a strained smile, she turned away to serve another customer, her cheerful face hastily back in place.

'She's a strong one, she is,' Bronwyn said, sadness in her eyes. 'It must tear her in two every time she visits Linda, then has to leave her.'

'Lily, Bronwyn, I'm so glad I've found you both,' Archie said before I had time to answer her. 'You're precisely the people we need. We've left it a bit late, but you were both so good in the last concert we put on. Will you audition for the panto we're doing? It's going to be *Mother Goose*.'

'But I was doing backstage stuff,' Bronwyn interrupted.

He patted her arm. 'We'll need your experience again, Bronwyn. I don't think we can be ready for a Christmas performance, but who knows? It might have to be in the new year.' He opened a bag he had with him and handed us both a sheaf of papers. 'This is the script. I hope it's funny.'

'Oh no, you don't!' Bronwyn said with a grin.

'Oh yes, I really do,' he quipped back. 'If you can help, think what you'd like to audition for. Bronwyn, you might like to be on stage this time. Up to you.' He closed his bag again. 'Right, let's see if there's anyone else here I can collar.'

He'd only taken a couple of steps when he turned back, his face serious. 'Lily, I suppose someone has told you about Grant, haven't they?' My stomach clenched, sure something bad was coming.

I was right.

'No, has something happened?'

'I'm afraid it has. He was in London and got caught in a bombing raid. He's in hospital.'

My heart seemed to stop. 'In the hospital? Grant?' I could hardly form sentences. 'Is he badly hurt?'

Archie bit his lip. 'I don't have any details. I only overheard a bit of conversation.'

Bronwyn's brain was working better than mine. 'How would we find out?'

Archie looked around, as if the answer might come from the surrounding drinkers. 'I'm not sure. You could try to discover who the head of his section is.'

'How do we do that?' Bronwyn asked. I'd had the same thought. With all the secrecy, we never even mentioned the names of our bosses. I knew Grant worked in the big house, but not where or what his job was.

'I suppose you'd have to ask the big boss's secretary,' Archie said.

Bronwyn took a sip of her drink, eyes searching for a solution. 'Our first day here, remember, we had to see the big boss to get told how to keep everything secret or else. We can find his office again.'

My limbs were shaky, and I struggled to stop my bottom lip from trembling. 'Will you come with me, Bron?'

She placed her arm round my shoulder. ''Course I will, silly.' With that, she downed the remainder of her drink and picked up her things.

As we walked the few steps to the big house, she tried to reassure me. 'It's probably nothing serious. Bet he's out again in a day or two.'

I always hated it when people made predictions like that based on nothing but unfounded hope. It was always done with good intentions, but didn't help at all.

We went up to the room we'd gone to on our first day and knocked on the door. There was no answer. We looked around wondering what to do. As we did, a woman carrying a load of files came out of another door. She realised who we were waiting for. 'You're out of luck. She's gone home. She's poorly.'

My heart sank, and I felt like collapsing on the floor.

'I understand my boyfriend is in hospital somewhere, and I'm trying to find out where he is. I don't know who else to ask.'

She blinked as she thought. 'I'm not sure who'd have that information. Perhaps the personnel girls?'

It took a further fifteen minutes until we found the right people to ask. 'I'm sorry, but we can't give out any personal information,' the man behind the desk said. He looked as if he couldn't care less about the welfare of people who worked there.

'But he's my boyfriend! We're engaged.' I pleaded, trying not to raise my voice. He was the sort of man who would accuse me of being hysterical.

'Your boyfriend?' he said with a sneer. 'Not his wife? In that case, I definitely can't disclose any information.'

With that, he waved us away and looked down at his paperwork as if we had already gone.

'Do you know his friends?' Bronwyn asked as we walked away from the horrible man. 'You must have seen him with people.'

I thought back to who I'd seen him with, but couldn't remember any names. 'Let's go back to the Beer Hut. Someone there might know. We'll ask everyone if we need to.'

Bronwyn caught my arm. 'I've got a better idea. I bet there are phone books in the library. Let's ring all the hospitals in the centre of London.'

She was right, of course, and we ran all the way to the library, my feet barely touching the floor. I was so agitated I stumbled over the request for help from the librarian on duty. She was very patient and soon told us which hospitals were our best bet. My hand shaking, I wrote the numbers on a scrap of paper she gave me.

'Quick,' I said to Bronwyn, 'have we got enough pennies for a phone call?'

We hadn't, but the kind librarian overheard our conversation and gave us all she had in her purse, another five pennies. I was so delighted I leaned over the counter and kissed her on the cheek. She was taken aback, but smiled and wished us good luck.

Running again, we went to the phone box in the hall. Luckily, no one was using it and I put my coins in the slot and dialled the number, pressing button A when someone answered.

'Can you advise me if Grant Frankland is a patient there, please?' I asked.

There was a pause. 'I'm sorry but we can't give out information like that. Are you a relative?'

My previous optimism faded. 'I'm his fiancée. Can you tell me if he's there, please?'

'I'm sorry, but if you're not a relative, I can't give out that information.'

I sensed she was about to hang up, so I quickly said, 'So you do know if he's there?'

'As I said, as you're not a relative, I can't give you that information. Please don't ask again.'

And with that, she hung up.

My shoulders slumped and tears formed in my eyes.

Bronwyn gave me a quick hug. 'Cheer up, I know exactly what to do.'

Ten minutes later Archie, the man who'd talked to us about the panto, was pressing button A.

'Good afternoon,' he said to the hospital switchboard. 'My name is Archie Frankland. Can you tell me if my son Grant Frankland is a patient there please? I'm terribly worried because I've heard he's been injured, but haven't been told what hospital he's in.'

We waited anxiously for several minutes as he pushed more pennies into the slot. 'They're checking,' he whispered.

He gave the phone his full attention again. 'Thank you so much, dear. Is he well enough to have visitors?'

Another pause, more pennies in the slot. He put his hand over the mouthpiece. 'They're transferring me to the ward to find out.'

The phone clicked. 'Good afternoon, my name is Archie

Frankland and I'm phoning about my son, Grant. Can you tell me what's happened to him, and if he can have visitors?'

He listened again, said 'Oh dear,' thanked the person he was speaking to, and said goodbye. He turned to me, looking very sombre.

'I'm afraid you need to prepare yourself, Lily.'

I held my breath, my heart thumping against my ribs.

'The good news is that Grant's life is not in any danger.' He paused.

'And the bad news?' Bronwyn said.

'I'm afraid the bad news is that his left leg has been amputated below the knee.'

I felt my legs go weak and Bronwyn put her arm round my waist to keep me upright. 'Poor dab. That's terrible. When can Lily go to see him?' she asked.

He sighed and his face dropped. 'That's the other bad news. He's refusing to see any visitors at all. Absolutely anyone, family or friends.'

* * *

'Gotta say, girl, you look right rough,' Bronwyn said when she saw me the next morning. I wasn't surprised. I hadn't slept a wink worrying about Grant. When I was an air raid warden, I saw what bombing did to people too many times to recall. The way the bombs and the damage they did tore into flesh, crushed skulls, severed limbs, leaving people dead or changed forever. Throughout the night, I kept getting horribly vivid pictures in my mind of Grant under fallen buildings or run over by a vehicle thrown into his path. What a terrible thing to happen to someone so lovely. And I was desperate to see him. Yet he didn't want to see anyone. Not even his loved ones.

'Do you think I should go to see Grant even if he doesn't want visitors?' I asked Bronwyn as we cycled to work. It was one of those lovely early November days, a clear blue sky, sunny and bracing air. It was totally out of sync with my mood.

Bronwyn grunted as she pedalled. 'Don't know what I'd do. You're in a right pickle. Why not write to him? You know where he is. If he writes back, you'll be clearer about whether to visit.'

It was a great idea, and I decided I'd write during my first break. Between lack of sleep and worrying about him, I worried I'd be useless use at work. There was no choice though and, miserable though I was, my work helped other people in worse situations. In the rare moments when I wasn't listening, I was mentally composing my letter to Grant. I'd tell him I loved him, of course, but needed to make him understand I'd feel the same way about him despite his injury.

I carried on with my work, only half there in my head, and hurried to write in my break. Paper was always in short supply, so I thought about every word before I wrote it. It took me the whole break time, and I didn't get a cup of tea. I was satisfied that although the letter wasn't perfect, it would convey my feelings. I'd post it later.

'You're probably not in the mood,' Bronwyn said in our afternoon break, 'but have you remembered it's auditions this evening?'

The panto had gone clean out of my head. 'I don't think I...' I began.

She took my arm. 'It's like this see, you moping around won't make Grant any better. It'll just make you worse. Come on, let's do the auditions. It'll take your mind off him for a little while.'

I'd briefly looked at the script and asked to be in the chorus. Some of those small parts had a little sentence or two to say, and that would be more than enough for me.

'Hey, Peggy's going to come. She'd be brilliant. Remember those saucy songs she sang one night at home? She's a natural. A panto is just her thing.'

She was right, and I hoped she'd go for a part big enough to showcase her talents.

I guessed the auditions would take less time than before, because some of the same people would be involved. Archie would know what parts they'd be good for.

'Are you going for a part this time, or stay backstage?' I asked Bronwyn.

She pulled a face. 'Don't you laugh now or I'll clock you one, but I thought I'd go for Fairy Goosedown, the magical fairy. Bet they've never had one my colour before.'

I tried to visualise her doing something so different from who she was, but that was what acting was about. 'Wow, that's a change for you. What will you do for the audition? You only get five or ten minutes.'

She tapped the side of her nose. 'What you don't know is I've spent every spare minute learning some of her lines. That's what I'm going to do.'

I tried to imagine her acting like a fairy, but totally failed. 'You kept that quiet. Good for you, I hope you get it. Is Carolyn going to audition? I haven't seen much of her lately, what with our different shifts.'

'And her being out with her bloke sometimes. But no, she's not interested, but listen to this – he is. He's going to audition and wants to play Mother Goose! He'll be the dame, all dressed up as a woman.'

My jaw dropped open. He could be fun, but it was impossible to imagine George dressed up as a pantomime dame.

I'd been to auditions before so I knew that would-be actors varied hugely at them. Some seemed to think they'd get a part just because they were posh or had an important job. Some gave completely the wrong piece, and that happened at this audition. One man went the whole hog with a long Shakespearean speech. He was good, but it didn't show Archie if he could do the over-the-top acting needed for a panto. One woman took too long with her piece and Archie cut her off mid-stream. She was outraged.

Bronwyn was amazing. She floated across the stage waving her arms like a fairy as she said her lines and wowed us all. I was sure she'd get the part. So would Peggy. She sang a saucy song I'd never heard before and did all the actions with it. She had us all in fits of laughter. Bronwyn was right. She was made for panto.

Archie dismissed us when we'd done our audition, but I waited for Bronwyn and Peggy. We were getting our coats on when George, Carolyn's boyfriend stepped on stage. Our eyes grew wider when we saw how different he looked. He must have been to the costume room and was already dressed as a dame, make-up and all. Overacting as panto demands, he knew all his lines, including calling to the imaginary audience for response. He was magic.

'Wow,' Peggy said as we walked to the Beer Hut. "'E'll get that part sure as eggs is eggs. I wonder if 'e's done acting before.' She put her arm through mine. 'You 'eard anything about your bloke, Lily? You must be right worried.'

Her question made my mood plummet again. 'I've heard nothing else, but I've written to him. We'll have to see.'

She squeezed my arm. 'Well, if it was me, I'd go there anyway. What's the worst that can happen? That's what I always ask meself. Worst is, you'll 'ave a wasted journey. That won't kill ya.'

* * *

The train was late, but I expected that. Like everyone else, I'd learned that travel in wartime was fraught with delays and cancellations. I stood on the platform, my shoulders hunched against the chill wind. I pulled my scarf tighter round my neck and was grateful that I'd put extra layers of underclothes on.

Peggy's blunt advice had played on my mind in the days since she'd given it. I'd had no reply from Grant, and decided I had nothing to lose except my day off if I went to see him. But I was full of trepidation, so much could go wrong. The trains might be cancelled, and Grant might refuse to see me.

Only half an hour past its due time, the toot-toot of the train told me it was coming. Travellers around me said goodbye to their loved ones, picked up their belongings and prepared to struggle to find a seat. Some people were in uniform, others civilians. I recognised two faces from the Park, but not people I knew. Boarding the train, I fought my way along corridors, stepping over sleeping squaddies and smooching couples. I'd almost given up hope of finding a seat when someone in the last carriage stood up and I grabbed his seat before anyone else could.

Lucky enough to sit next to the window, I tried to relax and feel optimistic about what was to come. The sun bathed the fields in its wintery light and naked branches of passing trees blew wildly in the fierce wind. At the next station, I shook myself out of my gloomy thoughts and got the panto script out of my rucksack. Thoughts of Grant prevented me from absorbing the words as I should, but even so, I could see some of the lines were hilarious. Acted right, they'd get heaps of laughs from the audience. I tried to picture my few lines, and the gestures I'd have to make, but worry about seeing Grant kept interrupting me.

My goal was to see him and let him know I still loved him, even with his injury, but he could refuse to see me, or ignore me as I sat next to him. Either thought made me feel demoralised.

How low he must be feeling to refuse visitors who might cheer him up.

The station master gave me directions to the hospital, and as I thanked him, I heard a rare noise. All the church bells in the city were ringing in amazing harmony. It was a wonderful sound, heart warming and comforting. I looked at the station master again. 'What's that about?' I asked.

His smile was wide. 'It's celebrating the victory at the second battle of El-Alamein. First time those bells've rung since May two years ago. Lovely noise. Gives you hope for the future.' Then another train pulling in got his attention, and I went on my way.

Walking through London brought back memories of living there, sharing rooms with Bronwyn. It had been an exciting and often terrifying time.

Finally, the hospital came into sight and I got butterflies in my stomach. I rehearsed what I was going to say to the ward staff if questioned. I was Grant's sister, come to see him. If he was still refusing visitors, I had no idea how I'd persuade them to let me see him though. I looked at my watch and was relieved I'd made it just right for visiting time. I went to the reception area to ask which ward he was in. When I stood at the ward door, I took a few deep breaths, glad other visitors were waiting to be let in too.

Hoping the nurses were too busy to notice me searching for the right bed, I walked in with the other visitors. They held gifts, and I kicked myself for coming empty handed. I must have looked at twenty beds before I spotted him, my fiancé. His back was to the door, and I had to walk around his bed to see him. I was shocked at how poorly he looked. His eyes were closed, and I could see he had lost a lot of weight and his skin had an unhealthy pallor.

'Grant,' I said softly, tenderly putting my hand on his shoulder, not sure if he was asleep or not. My hands were clammy and my chin wobbled.

There was no response.

I didn't dare make too much noise in case a nurse came to ask who I was. Cautiously, I bent over and kissed his cheek, then whispered his name. His eyes flew open, and he blinked fast when he saw me. At first he looked delighted, but then it was as if a switch had turned off in his eyes, in his brain.

'Go away!' he said, his voice harsher than I'd ever heard it.

I licked my lips and did my best not to cry. 'But, Grant, I've missed you so much.'

His eyes hardened still further. 'Go away, just go away!' And having said that, he turned his back on me. Nothing I did or said got any other response from him. Desperate, I sat beside him and tried to put my hand on his. He put his hand under the covers. I tried putting my hand gently on his shoulder, but he shook it off. Defeated, I continued to sit there for a further twenty minutes. All around me families and friends were chatting to other patients and one or two looked over at us curiously.

I spoke occasionally, telling Grant about life at Bletchley, about my small part in the panto, and that Peggy would be an aunt before long. Nothing brought a response.

After twenty minutes, I kissed him again on the cheek and walked away. As I neared the door I saw a nurse who must not have known he didn't want visitors. She didn't tell me off as I expected, instead she looked sympathetic.

'No luck getting him to talk?' she asked.

I bit my lips and shook my head, too upset to trust myself to speak.

'Don't blame yourself,' she said. 'It's not unusual when someone has an amputation or serious illness for them to turn away from others. They say it's something to do with them not feeling whole any more, not feeling worthwhile.'

'That's terrible. Does it ever pass?' I asked, my voice trembling.

She smiled and patted my arm. 'Usually, but there's no guarantee, I'm afraid. People who've suffered like him have emotional damage as well as physical.'

'How long will it be before he's discharged?'

She paused and thought for a minute. 'I think he's being sent to a hospital nearer home. Bletchley, isn't it?'

'That's where we work, not where he comes from.'

'Really? Well, he's being transferred to a hospital in Bletchley, I think. He does talk to me and he's very keen to get back to work. He wants to prove himself.'

His accident was so recent I couldn't imagine he'd be able to work any time soon. 'But...' I started.

'He's already begun learning how to use crutches. He's very determined. I don't know when he'll be transferred, though.'

I wanted to hug her. Grant may not be ready to speak to me, but if he was in a hospital nearer to me, it would be easier to visit him. Maybe in time he would change his mind.

But it wouldn't be easy.

3

It was a rare evening. All four of us were home at Happy Days at the same time. Peggy was sewing some pink ribbons on a dress she'd got at a jumble sale for little Linda. Carolyn was writing to her parents; Bronwyn was knitting and she was trying yet again to teach me how to knit. I was beginning to believe I'd never get the hang of it.

The radio was on, but we were only half listening until the newsreader announced that Hitler had made his annual speech in Munich on the nineteenth anniversary of the Beer Hall Putsch.

'What's the Beer Hall Putsch?' I asked.

'Sshh!' Carolyn said. 'Let's listen.'

The newsreader continued. 'Chancellor Hitler claimed that Stalingrad is now in German hands with only a few small pockets of resistance remaining.'

'Not what I've heard,' Carolyn said, then squealed and put her hand over her mouth. 'You didn't hear that. I never said a word.'

'What?' Bronwyn said. 'I didn't hear a thing, too busy trying to understand this knitting pattern.'

Before we could discuss it more, the telephone rang in the hall. I ran to answer it, hoping it would be Grant. Maybe he'd come out of his gloomy mood. But it wasn't him.

'Peggy! It's for you!' I shouted and left the phone on the hall table for her to pick up.

I went back into the living room and picked up three stitches I'd dropped from my knitting needle. 'Having this boring grey wool doesn't encourage me to knit,' I said. I'd bought a jumper full of holes at the jumble sale, and washed it three times to get the smell of mothballs out of it. Then I unpicked it and washed it again. Bronwyn showed me how to rewind it using the back of a chair.

She was watching my usual ineptitude. 'World War Three could have come and gone before you'll be able to knit gloves, or even a scarf come to that,' she said with a smile.

We could hear Peggy talking in the background, but not make out her words. Naturally, though, we were all keen to know what her call was about. We got precious few calls, and they usually meant something important had happened.

We heard her replace the handset, then she came back into the room with a strange look on her face. She looked excited, but worried at the same time.

'What's occurrin'?' Bronwyn asked.

Peggy plonked herself down on a chair. 'That was my sister, Marion. You know, I told you, she's in the family way. Thing is, she's not doing well, and the doc says she should take it easy till the nipper is born.'

'That's tough,' Carolyn said. 'Has she got someone who can help out?'

'That's the thing. There isn't anyone. Her old man is away at war and everyone else is working in factories or something.' She paused and bit her thumbnail. 'She wants me to have Linda.'

We were all silent, remembering that Linda was actually her daughter. On the one hand, Peggy would love spending more time with her. On the other, giving her back would be terrible. I could hardly imagine the pain that would cause.

'I can't 'ave 'er though, can I? Mrs W. wouldn't want a kiddie in the 'ouse making a mess, and who'd look after 'er when I'm at work?'

'Let's think about this,' Carolyn said. 'First, we don't know that Mrs W. would say no. I bet if you offered her extra rent, she'd be very keen.'

'And the school where I help little ones read has a nursery section,' I said. 'If we worked out our shifts, we could help you.'

She looked from one to another of us. 'You'd do that? For me? No kidding? It'd be terrific, and she could be with me for Christmas!'

'I'm used to looking after the little blighters with my family,' said Bronwyn.

'I've never looked after a child in my life,' Carolyn mused. 'But I suppose I could learn. If George and I get married, I expect he'll want children.'

'Yeah, but he'll afford a nanny, won't he!' Peggy said with a grin. 'You can just play at being lady of the manor.'

Carolyn pretended to swipe her.

Mrs W. usually came in at some point in the evening to check we were all behaving or hadn't cost her any money somehow. Only ten minutes later, we heard her door open and close, and the familiar sound of her smoker's cough.

'Evening, girls,' she said, squinting because of the cigarette smoke in her eyes. 'Nice to see you all together. But I've got to speak to you again about the soap. Someone is still leaving it in the water and it's going at an alarming rate.'

'But we buy our own soap in our bathroom,' I said.

'Yes, yes, I'm talking about the kitchen. You know how hard it is to get soap these days.'

Carolyn spoke up. 'Mummy sent me a couple of bars of soap. I'll put one in the kitchen. It's too good for the kitchen really, so I'll ask her to send cheaper stuff in the future.'

Peggy stood up, looking awkward. 'Mrs W., I'm glad you came now. I've got a favour to ask.'

Mrs W. frowned, blew her cigarette smoke away from us all, and looked at her. 'What's that then? Is it going to cost me any money?'

'No, it'll give you money,' Bronwyn chipped in.

Now Mrs W. perked up. 'What's that, then?' She sat down on the arm of the sofa, stubbed her cigarette out in the ashtray and lit up another one.

'It's like this,' Peggy started. 'My sister Marion is 'aving a baby, and the doc says she's gotta stay in bed or she might lose it. She wants me to have her little girl, Linda, for a few weeks.'

Mrs W. frowned again. 'A child? Here? How old is she?'

Peggy spoke so quickly her words were garbled. 'She's three and ever so well behaved.'

'Three? That's still the age for the terrible twos – temper tantrums and a lot of screaming. Me and Donnie don't want our peace disturbed.'

I almost choked. Our peace was regularly disturbed by the pair of them rowing. Sometimes we even heard things thrown at the wall. But Peggy managed to keep a straight face.

'She knows me well and I can try to get her in the nursery at the school. She can share my bedroom and I'll pay extra rent. I promise she won't disturb you.'

They haggled a price, then Mrs W. said, 'Well, I suppose I can help out. You know how much I like to help people. But she must be well behaved and no trouble to the others.' She looked round at us.

'Peggy asked us before she spoke to you,' I said, unpicking a stitch I'd done wrong. 'We'd all be happy to help her out. We can adjust our shifts so someone is always available.'

'Well, that's very generous of you.' She stood up and flicked her ash on the carpet, grinding it in with her shoe. 'Gets rid of the moths,' she muttered as she did every time we saw her do that.

When she'd gone, Peggy could hardly contain her excitement. 'My little Linda, with me!' She paused. 'Remember, girls, no one can know she's mine, especially Linda. I'm Aunty Peggy. And you can all be her aunties for a while, too.'

'When do you have to collect her?' I asked.

'As soon as possible, Marion said. The doc was really strict about it. I'm really worried for her. This'll be 'er first. Not that she doesn't treat Linda like 'er own. She's a great mum.'

I thought about my shifts. 'I'm free in a couple of days if you'd like some company getting her.'

Her smile got wider. 'Would you, Lil? That'd be great. Trying to keep an eye on a toddler what wants to be everywhere, and all 'er stuff is a bit 'ard.'

Carolyn folded up the letter she'd been writing and put it in an envelope. 'Well, I'm glad that's settled. I'm off to the postbox. I've asked Mummy to send me some more soap. Carbolic or something equally nasty. We need to keep Mrs W. happy.'

When she'd left, we went into the kitchen to make tea.

'I don't know if I should say this,' Peggy said as she got out the cups and saucers. 'But you know 'er bloke, George?'

Bronwyn and I nodded. 'What about him?'

'Well, I might be wrong, but I'm pretty sure I saw 'im

pinching another bloke's bum in the Beer 'Ut the other night. I think 'e thought no one else would 'ave seen 'im.'

I'd been filling the kettle, but stopped, trying to understand what she was saying. 'Pinched his bum? You mean they were messing about?'

She put the cups on the saucers with a thud. 'Didn't look like messing about to me. The other bloke would 'ave complained or laughed or something. But 'e didn't. In fact, 'e just smiled at George.'

Bronwyn whistled. 'Blimey. Not joking or nothing, but that makes you think he might be... well... you know... one of them blokes who likes men instead of women.'

I finally turned off the tap. 'But he can't be. He's going out with Carolyn.'

Peggy shook her head. 'You're an innocent one and no mistake. Some blokes like men *and* women. I've seen all sorts working in pubs. And some men they... well, they go out with women to cover up what they're really like.'

'If you'd grown up in a port like I did,' Bronwyn said, 'you'd think it was nothing unusual. When some blokes who were friends of Dorothy were drunk they forgot to be careful. I never know what I think of it. As long as they keep themselves to them-selves, it shouldn't harm anyone. But it's illegal, so it must be wrong.'

I sat down heavily on the chair. 'What the hell does being friendly with someone called Dorothy have to do with it? How come so many people know her?'

Peggy and Bronwyn looked at each other and grinned 'Oh, Lily. It's an expression. It means they, well, bat for the other team.'

My jaw dropped open and I felt like an innocent beside them.

'Blimey, That's news to me.' I thought for a minute. 'So Carolyn's boyfriend might not be being honest with her. What do we do?'

As I spoke, we heard the front door opening as she came back from posting her letter.

'Let's say nothing,' Bronwyn said. 'We need more information before we think about telling her. It might be nothing.'

4

'What number bus do we have to get?' I asked Peggy when we got off the train from Bletchley. The station at Euston was as crowded as ever. The smoke from the engines combined with cigarette and pipe smoke made our eyes water.

Peggy got out the letter from her sister, Marion. 'She says it's a number twenty-three and we can get it opposite the station.'

'When I was with the air raid people, I learned that all the Green Line coaches were converted into ambulances. Rumour had it that was planned for a year or more before the war started.'

'But they were pretending there wouldn't be a war then!' Peggy said, looking for a gap in the traffic so we could cross to the stop. 'Shows you can't believe a word what them political blokes say.'

We waited half an hour for the bus, getting colder and colder. We stamped our feet and rubbed our arms, but without much effect. When the bus came, it wasn't much warmer, but at least it was out of the biting wind. I was shocked at the state of it. Our seats, which would once have been padded and covered with material of some sort, were now wooden slats that left ridges in your bottom. I looked around and saw they weren't all like that, so I supposed it was just for those that needed repairing. And a window nearby had been replaced with wood, just a tiny triangle hole to see out of it. I thanked my lucky stars again that I was safe in Bletchley most of the time.

'How're you feeling about seeing your sister and picking up Linda?' I asked as we got going.

Peggy took a deep breath. 'Bit scared to tell you the truth. My stomach's in a knot. I just 'ope my sis ain't too bad. 'Course I'm excited, too. I 'aven't 'ad Linda to meself since she was a month old. She was such a lovely baby, pretty as a picture and good as gold. Broke my 'eart, it did, giving 'er up.'

I put my arm through hers and held her close to me. 'If only people weren't so rotten about having a baby when you aren't married. But the good thing is you'll have time to spend with her, and know her even better.'

She sighed again. 'And me 'eart'll break all over again when I 'ave to give 'er back. But I know it's for 'er own good.'

We stopped talking for a while, and I had a chance to look out of the steamy window. Barrage balloons floated above us, tethered to the ground to trap enemy aircraft. 'They call them Colonel Blimps,' Peggy said, looking at them. 'No idea why.'

Police constables with white armbands directed the traffic, and a road sweeper trundled on, searching for any worthwhile pickings.

'Look at them!' Peggy said, pointing to three women walking arm in arm. They looked straight out of a fashion magazine. 'I'd love to wear somethin' like that one day. I can dream!'

I didn't want to make promises I couldn't keep, but decided I'd look out for something for her in the next jumble sale. I could always alter anything I could find. I'd even once turned a man's jacket into a skirt. It was smelly and worn under the arms, but I managed to avoid those bits. With a wash, it looked good as new.

We turned the corner and were in a different world. The road had been bombed and a lot of the houses were flattened or half demolished. In one of them, the front had gone and you could see everything inside. It was like opening a doll's house with furniture, carpets, and beds untouched. You could even see the squares of newspaper they used for toilet paper hanging up on a wire hook.

'Poor sods,' Peggy said, looking over my shoulder. ''Ope they 'ave friends they can stay with.' I hoped they were alive.

Despite the damage, the market was still open and women queued for any food on offer. Anything to make the rations go round, even if it was black market. Peggy cried out, 'Oh, Lil, I should've brought something to give Marion, I'm empty-'anded. Whatever will she think?'

I tried to comfort her. 'Let's look for a shop when we get off the bus. But it's you she wants, not something you take. Anyway, because we're staying for the night, I've got a tin of corned beef and some bread in my rucksack.'

She smiled for the first time. 'You're right. Come to think of it, I've got a bit o' food in my pack too. There's a fish and chip shop near 'er. We can get some grub there.'

It was a relief to find her sister's street was untouched, probably because there were no important factories nearby. Kids were playing out in the street – football, skipping, off-ground touch and some lads pretending to be bombers. They ran around, arms outstretched, making aircraft noises, then shouting. *Boom, boom.*

As we approached the right house, a coal cart came along. 'You girls here to see Marion?' the driver asked.

'That's right. I'm 'er sister,' Peggy replied.

He hitched a bag of coal on his back. 'That'll cheer her up.

She's looked a bit down lately.' And with that, he lugged the coal round to the side of the house.

Marion's door was painted grey and was showing wear. The area round the keyhole was scratched, and the letter box needed a polish.

Peggy put her shoulders back and knocked. ''Ere we go,' she said, her voice a bit shaky.

Marion was a long time coming to the door and we could hear Linda shouting, 'Mum, there's someone at the door. Mum! Mum!'

When Marion opened it, I saw Peggy go pale. Marion was thin as a beanstalk, all skin and bones apart from her small pregnancy bump. Her skin was an unhealthy grey, but her eyes lit up when she saw Peggy.

'Peg! You've come! Am I glad to see you!'

She stood back so we could go in and followed us into the living room. Linda was bouncing around calling, 'Auntie Peggy. Auntie Peggy, did you bring me anything?'

Peggy bent down and picked her up. 'Of course I did, sweet-'eart. I'd never forget you, would I?' She opened her rucksack and took out a small bag of sweets. Linda threw her arms around her and kissed her wetly on her cheek.

Marion was still standing. 'I'll get you a cuppa,' she said.

'Oh no, you won't,' Peggy said, taking Linda's hand. 'Linda can 'elp me make them while you talk to Lily. She don't bite.'

Marion sat on the settee and tucked her legs under her. She cradled her small bump with care. 'It's good of you to come with Peggy. It would've been a 'andful with Linda an' all her stuff.'

'It's no problem. I expect she's told you we share a house with two other girls. We all help each other when we can. I'm so sorry you're having such a tough time.'

She got a hankie out of her pocket and blew her nose. 'First one, an' all.' She put her hand over her mouth. 'I shouldn't've said that. Linda can't never know. She's like she's me own, anyway.' She paused and looked down at her hands. 'I haven't told Linda about the baby, in case it goes wrong. Peggy knows, so if you an' your friends can keep it secret an' all, I'd be right pleased.'

We'd heard clattering from the kitchen and Peggy and Linda came in. Linda was proudly holding a plate with some bread and butter cut into neat triangles. It was at a dangerous angle, and I expected the bread and butter to be catapulted onto the lino any second. 'We ain't got no cake,' she said. 'This'll 'ave to do.'

Peggy smiled at me over her head and quickly rescued the plate. 'There's a clever girl, Linda.'

As we sat drinking our tea, Marion suddenly collapsed. She was conscious, but too weak to walk.

'What is it?' Linda asked, her face showing her terror.

Marion tried a smile. ''S nothing. 'Appens sometimes.'

Linda was busy drinking her milk and luckily seemed oblivious of the drama.

'What's the doc say?' Peggy asked, holding her sister's hand.

'Can't afford one, can I?' she replied, tears filling her eyes. 'I just saw 'im and I don't have money to see 'im again.'

Peggy's eyes grew wide. 'What, don't you belong to any friendly society what'll 'elp?'

'I ain't been able to keep up the payments, 'ave I?' Marion said. 'Just about got enough money for me rent and food, that's all. Doesn't 'elp that the rotten landlord put up my rent. The old man ain't bin paying me regular. I don't know where 'e is, neither. Ain't 'ad a letter from 'im for a few weeks. Still, I suppose they'd've told me if 'e was dead.'

Peggy told Linda to go and get her teddy from her bedroom – an excuse to have a conversation without her.

"Ow much does the midwife cost when you're 'aving it?'

Marion sighed. 'One and sixpence if I 'ave it at 'ome. More if I go into 'ospital. A lot more. Then I need to give you summat for looking after Linda.'

Peggy looked horrified. 'Don't be daft, girl.'

There was a tap on the back door, and it opened without waiting for a response. 'Cooeeee,' a voice shouted and in walked a plump woman with her hair in a scarf and wearing a flowery wrap-around pinny.

'Hello, Marion, am I interrupting anything?'

Marion tried to look more upright. 'Nothing that can't wait a minute, Flo. Were you after a cuppa? Peggy's just made one.'

Flo looked round. 'Sorry, Peggy, should have said hello. And who's this, then?' She smiled at me.

'I'm Lily, Peggy's friend.'

'Well, it's hello and goodbye from me, I'm afraid. Can't stop.' She produced a big bag. 'I had a bit of a collection from my family. You know, there's dozens of them. And this...' she held up the bag '...is a bag of clothes from newborns to about four years old. You might think some of them are only worth chucking, but I'll let you decide.'

Marion struggled to her feet and folded her arms round the woman. 'Oh, Flo. What would I do without you? You're like a mum to me.'

'I'd have loved to have a daughter like you, girl.' She waved goodbye and went back out the way she'd come. Linda had come downstairs and was listening to our conversation. 'Cor, Mum, is there some things for me in there?'

Peggy and I had planned to stay overnight because trains were so unreliable, and we didn't want Linda travelling when she was tired and irritable.

'Come on,' Peggy said. 'We've got all evening to sort this stuff out. Let's top up our cups. Bet there's some stuff we can pack for you to take to our house, Linda.'

Linda frowned. 'Do I call you mum when I'm with you?'

Marion paled, and Peggy looked as if she might weep. 'No, sweet'eart, your mum is still your mum, and I'm still your aunty.'

It was easy to see what that snippet of conversation had cost her. The colour drained from her face, and she gave Marion a long, painful look. Marion had sat down again, so I went over and put my arm round Peggy's shoulder. 'And I bet you're as brave as your Aunty Peggy, aren't you, Linda!'

She was already rummaging through the bag of clothes, but stopped briefly 'I am... I am... good,' she said. ''Ere, these are all too small for me!'

'That's because you've grown so quickly,' Peggy said, holding the big brown teapot. 'By the way, Marion, 'ave you got 'er identity card and gas mask?'

Marion nodded. 'They're all packed ready.'

While they'd been talking, I'd been worrying about Marion needing to see a doctor. 'Marion, don't take offence, but I want to pay for you to see a doctor.'

She started to protest, but I held up my hand. 'Please let me do this. I'm staying here overnight, eating your food and drinking your tea. Then when we go back, I'll have all the fun of playing with this little one.'

Marion looked at Peggy, who nodded. 'She's right, sis. I'll go and fetch the doc now. Won't be a mo, but who knows when 'e'll turn up.'

The doctor arrived an hour later. He examined Marion and said she needed better food and plenty of rest. Better food was easier said than done with rationing, but I nipped out to the shops with her ration book and bought what I could. We made a big stew, mostly vegetables and barley, but it fed us that night and would do for her the next day. It wasn't a lot, but it was something. All the while, Linda was chatting to her aunt in her childish way. I wondered how she would cope with being moved from everything she knew. At least Peggy would be the one constant in her life.

Peggy and I shared a bed that night and took ages to get to sleep.

'I'm torn,' Peggy said. ''Alf of me wants to take Linda back to Bletchley to give Marion a rest, but the other bit wants to stay 'ere to look after 'er.'

I could understand her feelings. I'd have felt the same. 'Will Flo and other neighbours help her out?'

'Yeah, they're a good lot, all 'elp each other. Seems like they all know what's going on.'

* * *

Amid many tears, we led Linda from her home after she'd given her mum hundreds of kisses. But it didn't take long once we got going for her to cheer up. Like a dog wants to sniff everything it passes, she wanted to comment on everything. 'Look, it's the milkman, isn't 'is 'orse big!' 'Coo, that dog's only got three legs.' 'There's mister postman! 'Ello, mister postman.'

It seemed she would never run out of steam.

'Don't worry,' Peggy said. 'She'll probably sleep on the train.'

On the way, we stopped at the newsagent's and bought Linda a *Dandy* comic to read. 'She can't read yet,' Peggy said. 'But she likes looking at the pictures and I can read it to her. It'll keep her quiet on the train.'

But not as quiet as she hoped.

At the station, Linda was overawed. She put her hands over her ears. 'I'm frightened, them trains is too noisy.' Despite already weighed down with Linda's stuff, Peggy picked her up and reassured her. Next, Linda was scared of the smoke from the train getting in her eyes, then the screech of the train wheels.

Her fear was quickly overcome with excitement when we got on the train, and she wanted to speak to all the other passengers. 'I like your 'at,' she said to one lady. 'Did you 'ave to kill a bird to get that feather?'

The woman looked daggers at her and muttered, 'Impudent child!'

I smothered a giggle.

Eventually, Linda settled a little and sat on Peggy's knee. It was then she noticed that the man opposite only had one arm. Her eyes grew bigger.

'Where's your other arm, mister?' she asked. Peggy and I wanted the ground to open up and swallow us. 'Did you lose it somewhere? My mum makes me look for things I've lost.'

He was old enough to be a veteran, so I guessed what his answer might be. 'You're a cheeky one, young lady. I lost my arm in France.'

'What's that, then?'

'It's another country. You have to go over the sea to get there.'

She paused for a minute, and I held my breath, wondering what was coming next.

'Can't you go back and get it?'

He laughed, and I was relieved he was so good about her nosy questions. But worse was to come.

'Can you wipe your bum, then? I need two 'ands. One to 'old me dress out of the way and the other to wipe me bum.'

I spluttered and put my hand over my mouth.

Luckily, he just grinned. 'I like a girl who asks lots of questions. That's how you learn. Yes, I can do most things, but it took me a while to get used to it, I can tell you.'

I thought of Grant and wondered if I dared speak to this kind man about him. But then I decided he could ignore me if he wanted to.

'My boyfriend has just had one leg amputated below the knee.' I was aware tears were forming in my eyes as I spoke. I still hadn't heard a thing from Grant, even though I'd written every day. Every day I hoped to hear from him, and every day with nothing from him, my heart broke a little more.

'That's tough. How's he coping?'

'I don't really know. He won't talk to me or answer my letters.'

He nodded and leaned over to pat my hand. 'He'll come round, Love, never you fear. It takes a lot to get used to not being who you were before. Give him time, and a lot of patience.'

The train whistle hooted, and he looked out of the window. 'Oh, that's my stop.' He gathered his belongings together. 'It's been nice speaking to you, ladies. And you, young girl, keep asking those questions.'

Eventually, Linda went to sleep, and I had time to ponder on what the man had said. He'd been in a similar situation to Grant regarding his injury, and probably been in the trenches too, experiencing untold horrors. I wondered if he'd had someone waiting for him to come back safely from war. Someone who loved him as much as I loved Grant. Someone who prayed for him every night, who listened to the radio and read the newspapers with fear in their heart. Grant was safe. He wasn't miles away at sea, or fighting hand to hand or in the air. Even so, he was suffering dreadfully, and I despaired of knowing how to help him.

But then I thought about the man in the carriage, the man who had overcome the dreadful injury and found a way to enjoy life again. It gave me an idea of how to bring Grant round.

It could go horribly wrong, but I had to try.

* * *

That evening, Peggy took Linda up to bed after a bath and something to eat. They were going to share a bed, but it was too early for Peggy to sleep. She was upstairs ages, and I heard a good deal of crying and 'I want my mummy!', 'You're not my mummy!'

When Peggy eventually came down, she looked exhausted, dark rings round her eyes. 'I thought she'd never go to sleep,' she said, her voice as weary as her face.

We went into the kitchen and I made her a cup of cocoa. 'This is hard for you,' I said. 'I noticed you seemed a bit up and down about being close with Linda today.'

She looked up sharply. 'What d'ya mean?'

'Don't think this is a criticism, it's not. Sometimes you were very close, hugging her and kissing her, other times it was as if you wanted to pull away. Perhaps you were just tired.'

She took a sip of her cocoa and sat back. 'Truth is, Lil, I'm scared to get too close. When she was born, I looked after 'er full time for a few weeks and got to love every inch of 'er, every finger, every toe, everything. I stayed in a mother and baby 'ome. 'Artless place it was. Run by nuns. You'd think they'd be kind, being religious and all. Didn't beat us or nothing, but weren't kind, not even after giving birth. Never a kind word. And some of the girls 'ad 'ad a baby before. They got a lecture every day and called all sorts of names by the nuns.'

I tried to imagine having a mindset to be so cold and unfeeling towards girls in need, most of them young and scared. I found it impossible to imagine.

I got up and put on some more milk. Another cup of cocoa seemed called for. I dug around and found a couple of biscuits, too.

'They tried 'ard to make me give 'er up for adoption, went on and on at me, pushing the forms under me nose,' Peggy went on, 'but I weren't 'aving none of it.'

My heart went out to her. 'That must have been so hard.'

She nodded. 'You're not kidding. I breastfed 'er and looked after 'er every minute of the day or night.' She paused and bit her lip. 'And stupid idiot that I am, I kept 'oping against 'ope that my boyfriend would come back to me and we'd get married. I shoulda known better. 'E was rubbish through and through.' She got up and washed her cup. "E'd've made a lousy dad, too.'

'Didn't you have to pay to stay in the home?' I was aware of asking too many questions and didn't want to upset her, but she seemed happy to talk.

'That's right, we did. We got some from the National Assistance Board. The dads were supposed to pay too. Fat chance! If they coughed up, they'd be admitting it was their kiddie. Most of 'em ran a mile.'

'So how did Marion end up taking Linda?' I asked.

She bit her lip again and sighed. 'She never told me, but it was always in 'er mind if I couldn't keep the baby. They 'adn't 'ad much luck 'aving one. But she didn't want to get my 'opes up, so she didn't mention it till she'd 'eard from 'er 'ubby.'

'That was pretty sensible of her. It would have been awful if he'd come home and then said he didn't agree. What took them so long to decide?'

"E was away fighting, wasn't 'e, and letters weren't getting through. She waited and waited for an answer. Lucky for me, one came just in time. You can only stay so long in them 'omes then they throw you out.'

'I suppose they must look after a lot of girls in your position. They must need every bed,' I said, locking the back door.

'Yeah, that's right. Anyways, 'e come up trumps and said 'e'd take my little baby in. They've moved since and none of the neighbours know Linda isn't theirs.'

* * *

I'd been surprised by Mrs W.'s reaction when she first met Linda. Depending on her mood and how much alcohol she'd had, her response to anything could vary.

'Oh, you little sweetie!' she said when we walked in. Linda, a little nervous with someone new, especially someone as strange as Mrs W., was holding back.

'Shy, are you!' Mrs W. said, then bent over to kiss her cheek, moving her cigarette away so the smoke didn't go in the little girl's face. It was surprising the smell of strong spirits didn't knock her out though.

Linda would have stepped back at this enthusiastic approach from a stranger if Peggy hadn't been standing immediately behind her.

Mrs W. looked from one to the other. 'Peggy! This little treasure looks exactly like you. You could be her mother!'

'She's not my mum,' Linda said, rather crossly. 'She's my auntie.'

'Yes, yes,' Mrs W. said, 'but you look so much like her.'

Peggy had gone pale and the smile on her face was fixed and didn't reach her eyes. 'It's not surprising if she looks like me, after all, 'er mum's my sister and me and her look like each other.'

'Come with me,' Mrs W. said, and taking Linda's hand led her to the kitchen. 'I expect you could eat a biscuit, all little girls like biscuits.'

Linda's face brightened. 'Yes, please, lady. I like biscuits. I like cakes an' all. 'Ave you got one for me?'

Peggy and I looked at each other, wondering how Mrs W.

would react to this. She was very careful about expenditure. 'No cakes today, little one, but perhaps another day.'

We took off our coats and went into the kitchen. For the first time I became conscious of how thin Linda was. After years of rationing, we were all thin, but her arms and legs were like sticks. I wondered if her mother had been too broke to buy much food, or perhaps too unwell to cook nutritious meals. I resolved to talk to Peggy about fattening her up.

But if Linda's forthrightness was embarrassing, worse was to come.

Mrs W. poured a glass of water and leaned over her to put her glass on the table. She looked at Linda's head and gave a little scream.

'Nits! She's got nits!'

She was right. I couldn't understand how neither Peggy nor I had spotted it. I immediately wanted to scratch my head and saw that the others did, too. Linda didn't have so many that her hair seemed to move around. I'd seen that on some of the children at the school where I helped a boy learn to read. But you only had to separate a few strands to spot them.

Mrs W. was backing away. 'You'll have to get rid of them, or she'll have to go.'

Linda, who'd hoped for a second biscuit, looked about to cry, her bottom lip trembling. I stepped in. 'We'll deal with it,' I said. 'I expect you can spare a cup of paraffin and I'll go to the chemist's in a minute and get a nit comb.'

Mrs W. had lit another cigarette, clinging to it as if it would keep the nits at bay. 'You'll have to keep checking, once might not be enough! I remember when my lad had them...' she stopped mid-sentence. 'When some boys at my lad's school had them, other mums told me about it.'

With that, she hastily backed away. 'Let me know when they're gone,' she said, leaving by the back door.

* * *

Linda alternated between being happy and being sad and clingy. Peggy managed to change her shifts to get a couple of days free and arranged for Linda to start at the nursery class the next week. She took her to the park, read to her and played games, but nothing seemed to cheer her up.

'She'll get over it,' Mrs W. said, still keeping her distance despite Peggy's assurance that the nits were gone. 'She'll just need a bit of time.'

We often talked about her mothering advice. While much of it was good, we kept in mind that her only son was in prison. *Innocent as the day he was born*, she said frequently, but we knew better.

'Are you sure you're okay looking after her?' Peggy asked me next day. 'I feel bad leaving her with you.'

'She'll be fine, won't you, Linda? We'll have fun.' Linda looked unconvinced and clung to Peggy's legs.

'Tell you what, Linda,' I said. 'We'll go to the clinic and collect your orange juice and malt. You like that, don't you?'

She stuck out her bottom lip. 'I ain't 'aving no oil.'

I couldn't blame her. It was disgusting. 'No, no cod liver oil.' I didn't tell her the government had hidden it in the delicious malt after widespread dislike of it. What she didn't know would do her the world of good.

Twenty minutes after Peggy left, Carolyn came in from her night shift. Usually immaculate, she had dark rings round her eyes and her shoulders sagged. 'I'll have a cuppa before I go up,' she said. 'It's been busier than ever last night.'

I longed to ask her what her work involved that made it busier. Was there some important war happenings the rest of us would only find out about later? Or not at all? I looked forward to the days when we'd be able to talk about our work, but it wouldn't be while we were at the Park.

'Linda and I were just going in the kitchen and she's going to help me make a Christmas pudding, aren't you?'

Her eyes lit up. 'Pudding? Can I lick the bowl?'

'We'll make you a cuppa, too,' I assured Carolyn.

The government had issued a pudding recipe fit for wartime. I put on the kettle and Carolyn kept Linda amused while I gathered the ingredients: plain flour, baking powder, nutmeg, cinnamon, mixed spice, suet, sugar, breadcrumbs, marmalade, eggs and stout.

Carolyn watched with interest. 'We always have brandy in ours at home. I used to watch Cook making it. She let me have a stir.'

I put tea leaves in the pot. 'Brandy indeed. As Bronwyn would say, there's posh you are! We only ever had beer.'

'Where did you get all this lot from? It's a wonder Mrs W. hasn't claimed it.'

I tapped the side of my nose. 'Loose tongues lose us the war!' I said with a grin. In fact, I'd persuaded the cooks at the Park to give me the spices and had been collecting the other bits for ages. I'd hidden them in the bedroom to keep them safe.

'The other thing we always have is a sixpenny bit.' She dug around in her bag and produced one. 'There, that is my contribution to the meal.'

'Will I get it?' Linda said, hopping from one foot to the other.

'We'll see,' I said. There was a good chance she'd still be with us at Christmas, but nothing was certain.

'How's it going with George?' I asked when I'd poured the tea.

'We're like ships that pass in the night,' she said, taking a sip. 'I almost wish I'd joined in the pantomime group. I'd see more of him then. I'm still not sure how I feel about him, really. Early days.'

He'd certainly been to every rehearsal and obviously enjoying camping up his role. He was a natural. Every time I bumped into him around the Park, it was all he talked about. I hadn't thought of it before, but he talked about that a lot more than he talked about Carolyn.

As we were speaking, I was following the recipe, giving Linda as much to do as she was able. 'Do you see you and him going places?' I asked Carolyn.

She leaned forward and put her chin in her hand. 'I'm not sure. In many ways he's ideal. We come from the same background, have some of the same friends, but...'

I waited. 'But...'

She shook her head. 'We'll wait and see.'

It was a relief that she wasn't as committed as I'd thought. If he did turn out to prefer men, it would make it easier to tell her. But there was still a chance that we'd got that idea all wrong.

'What about Grant? Is he getting better? I heard he'll be back at work very soon.'

I had an idea that I hoped would help Grant and would also allow Carolyn to spend more time with George. 'If the panto group agree, I hope we can put on the show for local veterans. The men who were in the last war.'

'That's a great idea, but how could I get involved and how will it help Grant?'

Linda was waving her arms around. 'Can I lick the bowl now, Auntie Lily?' I scooped every bit I could into a bowl and handed her the rest to eat. Then I replied to Carolyn's question.

'It might go horribly wrong, but I'm hoping that when he sees all those men, some of whom have terrible injuries and have got on with their lives, he'll feel more positive about his own future. But I'm worried about having enough time to organise it all.' I gave a cheeky grin. 'You're a brilliant organiser. I've heard you talk about organising charity dos for your mother and all sorts. It'd be great if you took that on. And then you'd see more of George, too.'

I was distracted by Linda tugging at my apron. 'I need a wee! Now!' She grabbed my hand and pulled me out of the kitchen. By the time we came back, Carolyn had finished her tea and was ready to go to her bedroom.

'Okay, I'll do it, but how any of us will find time what with work and looking after this little one, I have no idea. Still, we'll manage somehow.'

Linda had been listening. 'I'm goin' to school next week, Aunty Peggy said. I'm a big girl.'

'So you are,' Carolyn said, and ruffled her hair. Linda glared at her and straightened it again.

Linda watched as I put the pudding on to steam. 'Right, shall we play Snap?' I said. We played for a few minutes, but she soon got bored.

'I've got an idea for after we've been to the clinic,' I said. 'We'll ask Mrs W. to keep an eye on the pudding and go to the pictures. *Dumbo* is on.'

Her eyes were round as saucers. 'Pictures? I've never been to the pictures, but Mum told me about it. What is *Dumbo*?'

By the time I'd explained, she was jumping up and down with excitement. I worried though that I'd given her so many new experiences in one day that she'd expect that all the time.

* * *

What I hadn't counted on at the cinema was what was on before the gentle Disney film. Pathé News showed Nazis marching at a parade; their black, white and red uniforms seemed to leap off the screen, and the sound of their jackboots on the concrete reverberated throughout the cinema. Initially aghast and silent, many people in the audience then stood up and hurled abuse at the screen, loud and furious, fists shaking in the air. Unable to understand what was happening, Linda was frightened, and sat on my knee trembling.

I'd warn the others to take her after the news if they took her to the cinema in future.

5

Cycling past the shops on the way from home to the hospital, I was relieved Grant had been moved to a local one. I thought again of the differences between Bletchley Town and London. When I'd lived in London, it was exciting, with dance halls, cinemas, clubs and endless cafés. On the rare occasions I had free time, there was plenty of entertainment to choose from. The downside was the bombing in what was being called The Blitz. Nine months of what seemed like non-stop bombing, countless people dead, homeless, or their lives changed forever.

Bletchley Town couldn't have been more different. No bombing, but instead a massive influx of children who were evacuated from London and other cities targeted by the Nazis. The schools had never had more children and had to deal with little ones from very different backgrounds. Although the town had a lot less to offer in the way of entertainment than London, those of us who worked at Bletchley Park had plenty of choice. Dances, clubs, sports, choirs, all sorts of activities were on offer all week. The problem was getting to them when you worked shifts.

I stopped to let a horse and cart go by, admiring the beautiful hard-working animal. With petrol hard to come by, they were still commonly seen. As often happened, this one had a little lad running behind it. He was carrying a bucket and a garden spade.

'Getting plenty of manure?' I shouted.

He grinned. 'Yes, missus, I got three gardeners wanting it. That's my pocket money for the week.'

My thoughts turned to the last time I'd been out with Grant. We'd seen a film shown at the Park, but for the life of me, I couldn't recall what it was. But I remembered sitting in the dark holding his hand, smelling his woody cologne, snuggling up to him. It had been a long time since I'd felt that content with anyone.

By the time I arrived at the hospital where Grant was a patient, I was so cold my fingers had gone blue despite the gloves Bronwyn had knitted me for the previous Christmas. As I walked in I was struck by the familiar hospital smell. Antiseptic, with suggestions of soaps and cleaners. Nurses, doctors and porters walked here and there, purposeful, professional.

An ambulance pulled up outside, its siren blaring. I looked around, wondering where to go, nervous about seeing my love again. A priest walked past looking exhausted, and I wondered how many patients he had to comfort each day. How many last rites he had to give. Nevertheless, he saw me hesitate and stopped to talk to me.

'You'll find the reception desk over there,' he said and pointed to my right. In my nervousness, I'd completely missed it. I thanked him, swallowed hard and walked towards it.

'I'm looking for Grant Frankland,' I said. 'Can you tell me what ward he's on, please?'

The receptionist looked at the clock. It was five minutes to visiting time, and she smiled for the first time. She consulted some lists on her desk. 'He's in ward nine. It's down the corridor behind me on the left. By the time you get there, they should be opening the ward for visitors.'

My heart wanted me to run down the corridor to see him, but my head slowed me down. What if he still wouldn't speak to me? What if he was worse and had given up altogether? What if he finished our relationship? Fear made my mouth dry and my stomach clench. Should I wait until he responded to my letters or risk a second rejection?

I got to the ward door just as the sister opened it. My indecision was solved by being carried in on a wave of other visitors anxious to see their loved ones. As I walked between the beds, my gaze swivelled from man to man, looking for the man I loved. The ward was pristine, nothing out of place. Every bedcover was so smooth it was as if there was no patient in it. One chair waited beside each bed, sandwiched between that one and the next. As one patient I passed sat up, he coughed and clutched his chest. Another had both legs in plaster, a third had a massive bandage around his head. Some slept while their visitors waited patiently for them to wake up. So much sadness in one room, but also so much hope for recovery.

I walked up and down twice, but couldn't see Grant, although eventually I found an empty bed. I looked at the clipboard with patient notes attached to the bottom and saw it was his. Alarmed, I hurried over to the sister's desk. 'I'm here to visit Grant Frankland,' I said, so breathless I could hardly speak coherently.

She looked up and smiled. 'He's having physiotherapy at the moment. You can go there if you like. He should be finished soon. It's two doors down on the left.'

Relief that he was still alive allowed my shoulders to drop and my racing heart to return to normal. I turned, and all but ran down the corridor, almost crashing into a porter pushing a trolley full of boxes. There was a small window in the physio-therapy room and I peered in, anxious about what I would see.

My heart went out to Grant as I watched him unseen. He was practising using crutches, his right trouser leg folded over and pinned up. A reminder of what had happened to him as if he would ever forget. His eyebrows were lowered, his eyes squeezed, his nose wrinkled, and his mouth slightly open as he struggled to breathe through the pain. A door nearby banged, and he started, his head jerking up, eyes wide. Sweat appeared on his forehead.

Remembering the ward sister said he'd be finished soon, I decided to wait, watching the physiotherapist give him encour-agement after his fright. Only when he collapsed into a wheel-chair did I knock on the door and walk in.

'Hello, Grant,' I said, trying to sound as if there was nothing wrong between us. 'Can I push you back to your bed?' I tried to kiss his cheek, but he pulled away from me.

His eyes narrowed and his jaw tightened. 'No thank you, Lily. I can do that for myself,' he said, his voice harsh as nails on a chalkboard. The physio watched in dismay as he pushed the wheelchair past me, struggled to open the door, and left.

She came over and touched my arm. 'I'm sorry he was like that. If you can spare a minute, I'll explain what we often find with people in his position.'

I agreed, and we sat together in a corner of the cold clinical room.

'When someone has a terrible injury,' she said, 'those of us who've never experienced something like that find it difficult to understand their behaviour. Their reluctance to seek help, even from their loved ones. The thing is, and it's hard to explain, they often are picturing what happened to them in their mind. Do I understand he was caught in a bombing incident?'

'That's right. I wasn't with him, but someone told me he was half buried for ages before he was rescued. It must have been awful.'

She nodded. 'So he'd have been in unbearable pain, trapped, unable to help himself. He must have been bleeding profusely and getting weaker and weaker. I'm guessing he's usually someone who is independent. So being helpless is part of the problem, but then there's the fear he'll die before they free him.'

'I used to be with the air raid people,' I said. 'I know how awful it is. He probably saw other people injured or worse. I saw it time and time again and was knocked unconscious myself once. I'll never forget it. Those pictures will stay in my mind for ever.'

The phone in the corner of the room rang and, excusing herself, she went to answer it. While she was gone, I remembered not only the time when I and the man I loved were bombed, but other times. Times when I saw children dead, missing limbs, horrific burns and too many people made homeless to count. I wondered if that dreadful man Hitler would ever pay for what he'd done to so many innocent people. Mr Churchill was not saying the war was nearly at an end. It was hard to feel hope for a brighter future. And what if the Nazis won and came over the English Channel? We'd be under their rule, and from what I heard at work, it was terrifying. Even ordinary Germans and French people lived in fear of the brutal soldiers, their lives dreadfully restricted.

The physio apologised when she got back and continued, 'I was saying, so people that injured often don't want to talk about it because it brings back the awful pictures, and the overwhelming feelings with them.'

'But surely he could talk to me,' I said, struggling not to cry.

'It's understandable that you'd think that, but talking to you will bring it all back just the same. The last thing he'll want to do is look weak in front of you. Added to all that, your boyfriend has to adjust to life without half his leg. That's enormous. He's likely to feel it's not just some physical part of him that's missing, but who he thinks he is. Some people sail through it, but for others, mental recovery can take a long time.'

I sobbed and wiped my eyes. 'I feel so useless.' I sniffled. 'I want to help him, but he won't let me.'

She put her arm round my shoulder. 'Give it time, just keep offering. Most people come round with time, but there's no way of knowing how long. By the way, he's very determined to go back to work quite soon.'

'Surely not!' I said, feeling alarmed. 'He's not well enough.'

She shook her head. 'I certainly hope he'll give himself longer to recover, but he tells me he has a desk job. At least he won't have to struggle on his crutches too much. Maybe work is what will bring him out of himself, feeling useful, part of the war effort.'

I thanked her for her kindness and left the room. But I stood outside in the corridor for a while, doing my best to compose myself and decide what to do. After that rejection, I was scared to go to see Grant, but there wasn't much visiting time left so I had to make a quick decision. Taking a deep breath, I strode down the corridor again and went straight to his bed. He looked up, then looked away.

Despite the poor reception, I sat beside him and put my hand on his. He didn't pull it away, and I hoped that was a good sign. He was sitting in bed, a wire cage over his legs under the top cover, but every muscle in his body was tense, as if he didn't dare let himself relax.

'I know you don't want me to be here,' I said, keeping my voice low and warm. 'I love you, Grant, and I need to know you're okay.'

'Well, I'm not,' he muttered, almost under his breath.

I moved so I could look at his face, even though he carried on avoiding eye contact. 'Grant, something awful has happened to you, but I still love you just as much as before. You're still the man I fell in love with. Still the man who is kind and thoughtful, who is doing important work to help bring this war to an end. Nothing will change how I feel about you.'

He didn't look up, but I felt him squeeze my hand for a second. I lifted his hand to my lips and kissed it, then I leaned forward and kissed him on the cheek. 'You're still my special love,' I whispered.

I don't know if he would ever have replied, but at that moment the sister rang the bell. 'Visiting time over! Time to leave!'

'I'll visit you again next time I'm on the right shift,' I said, and kissed his cheek again. He didn't reply, but at least he didn't pull away this time. As I left the ward, I looked back, but he was still sitting unmoving. I didn't know whether to feel hope for our relationship or not. He hadn't flinched, but he hadn't really responded beyond that small squeeze of the hand. I decided to keep writing to him and hope my other idea for bringing him out of himself would work.

* * *

The shops were beginning to have Christmas decorations in their windows, a bit early as it was only 2 December. It's not as if any of them had much to sell. That meant that we had to get our thinking caps on to find something to give our friends and family.

'Come on,' Bronwyn said. 'There's another jumble sale on.

Last one before Christmas. Let's see if we can grab a bargain.' She looked down at her plimsolls.

'I could do with some new daps, too, if we can find any my size. These are letting in water.'

For December, it was a lovely day. Bright blue sky with hardly a cloud, but cold. So cold it seeped through all my layers of clothes, wriggling its way into seams and zips. Exposed skin on my face glowed, but after a night shift and a good sleep, I was ready for some fresh, crisp air.

Bronwyn looked at her watch. 'Come on, we've got time to walk there through the park.'

The trees were naked, branches waving around as if trying to get attention. There were still a few fallen leaves huddled together round some trees, their bright autumn colours faded and sad. A dog off its lead was running around chasing birds without success. Ducks, who never seemed affected by weather, swam around or walked across the grass looking for something to eat.

On the other side of the park was the children's play area with some swings and a roundabout. 'Gotta own up,' Bronwyn said, rubbing her hands together to keep them warm. 'I suggested coming this way 'cos I know Thomas brings his daughter here sometimes on a weekend.'

'You haven't mentioned him lately. Last time was when you were going to a café with him. How did it go?'

She paused. 'Okay, I think. He's a nice bloke, really different from the type I usually go for—'

'He's single for a start!' I interrupted with a grin.

She thumped my arm. 'Not kidding or nothing, but if we live to be a hundred, you'll still be reminding me of that.'

I felt guilty and put my arm through hers. 'You're right. I promise not to mention your wicked past again!'

'Anyways, before you were so mean to me, you were asking how we'd got on. He's easy to talk to and a really kind person. There's no great electricity between us, but I think it could grow. There's no rush. This damn war isn't going to be over any time soon, so we'll both be here for a while.'

'What about his daughter? How are you getting on with her?'

'Bella? Haven't seen her enough, really. I'm hoping this walk'll give us a chance to bump into them.'

We were almost too late. As we arrived, Thomas and his daughter were preparing to leave. Her face was red from being pushed through to cold air on the swing.

'Bronwyn!' Thomas said when he saw her. 'How nice to see you! What are you doing here?'

'Me and Lily are off to the jumble sale.' She turned to Bella. 'Hello, you must be Thomas's daughter. He told me how pretty you are and he was right.'

Bella didn't answer. She simply grabbed her father's hand and tried to pull him away.

'Don't be rude, Bella,' he said. 'We won't be a minute.'

'Do you like jigsaw puzzles?' Bronwyn asked the girl. 'If I see one at the jumble sale, I'll get it for you.'

The girl didn't answer, but the angry frown on her face lightened and she stopped pulling on her father's hand so hard.

'She's a bit shy,' he said. 'I'm sure she'd like a jigsaw puzzle if you see one.'

Bronwyn squatted down, so she was on a level with Bella. 'I can't promise, but I'll do my best, and if I find one, I'll give it to your dad. Okay?'

Bella gave a brief nod in reply, but still refused to look at Bronwyn. It was a long way from acceptance, but Bronwyn hoped it was a start.

When we'd said goodbye to Thomas and his daughter, we

continued towards the church hall where the jumble sale was being held.

'She's a bit young for jigsaw puzzles,' I said. 'Does she even know what they are?'

Bronwyn stopped to pick up a child's shoe that had been left on the grass. 'Someone'll be tamping to lose that. They cost a bomb.' She paused. 'I know she likes jigsaw puzzles because Thomas told me he'd managed to find some with only a few pieces. Not only that, he's pasted some suitable pictures from magazines onto cardboard and cut out the shapes.'

My eyes brightened. 'Then if we don't find anything suitable, we can do the same. It sounds simple enough. You looking for anything else at the sale?'

'Just daps, but you never know what you'll find.'

We were a couple of minutes early, but the queue outside the church hall was already quite long. Mostly women, mostly middle aged, but some older and some older men, too. At the back of the queue were a couple of mothers pushing their children in pushchairs.

'Wish we'd come sooner, *cariad*,' Bronwyn said. 'We'll have to scout round quick if we want to get some bargains. I'm going to look for those daps, then some jumpers to unpick. What are you after?'

'A winter coat. Mine's almost threadbare.'

When the doors opened, people rushed in as if they were running away from a sinking ship. The organisers had helpfully put signs on the wall, saying what each table held and that saved a lot of bother. I headed to women's coats, but they all seemed too small or too full of moth holes. Undaunted, I hurried over to the men's coats' table. An elderly man, thin as a rake, was trying on just what I'd hoped to find. *Please don't buy it*, I said to him without words. My luck was in. He took it off and put it back on the table. When he saw me pick it up, he shook his head. 'Too old, love, you won't want that one.'

But I did.

I could see it was good quality wool even though with age it had become bobbly. The lining had some small tears in it, but it had all its buttons and I couldn't find any moth holes.

'You're never going to buy it,' said the old man, who was still sorting through the coats on offer. 'Wasting your money, you are. You young girls!'

I grinned at his attitude. 'Look inside the fabric. It's not bobbly like the outside. I'm going to unpick the whole thing and turn it inside out. Then I'll get a dressmaking pattern and make a coat to fit me.'

His jaw dropped open. 'Ain't you the clever one? You can do all that?'

'I can, even if I am a young thing!'

I handed over my money and went to see what else I could find. Bronwyn had found the plimsolls she was looking for and was searching through the jigsaws for something for Bella. While she did that, I looked through the pile of books and found a couple that I thought might be right for her age. One was big with beautiful illustrations. Some of them would be ideal for home-made jigsaws.

I found some bits and pieces that, with a bit of creativity, could be turned into Christmas decorations. It would be fun to make them with Linda.

Would this relationship work for Bronwyn, I wondered. In all the time I'd known her, she'd never had a serious one. She'd enjoyed playing the field, though.

Maybe things were changing for her. I hoped so. She deserved it.

* * *

Next day, we had our first panto rehearsal. Bronwyn and I wished we'd spent more time learning our lines, not that I had many. She'd got her wish to be the magical fairy and, although she wouldn't admit it, was terrified. The last time she'd been on stage was as a sheep in her school nativity play.

'Right,' said Archie, when we'd finally all arrived and settled ourselves down. He'd put markers on the floor for where we had to stand at different stages, and chairs to substitute for furniture that would be there for the real thing. As first rehearsals go, it was a disaster.

Two men were playing the cow. Watching them get into their costume was a pantomime on its own. They kept falling over and giggling like kids. When they finally got the two halves together, there was a fart so loud, they probably heard it in the town. The back end of the cow quickly undid itself from the front and emerged frantically waving away the smell. He still wore his cow legs.

'Do that again, and I'll kill you!' he shouted to the head, who was still in his costume as well and whose face couldn't be seen. He was shaking with laughter. Outraged, the rear end kicked him over, still swearing. The front end of the cow fell off the stage and had to be helped up, cursing and swearing.

Two people had done no practice at all, and had to read their lines from their script. They earned a telling-off from Archie.

Although it wasn't a dress rehearsal, a few people were already in their outfits including Carolyn's boyfriend George. As the pantomime dame, his dress was bright emerald green and outrageously silly with heaps of multicoloured frills and flounces. Although he didn't have make-up or a wig on, he still acted the part and had us all in fits.

'Think he likes wearing women's clothes?' Bronwyn whispered to me.

Bronwyn's fairy needed some work, but she did brilliantly for a first rehearsal and got a pat on the back from Archie. I watched her, amazed – the part was so different from her normal self.

'I think you've missed your calling,' I said when we were preparing to leave. 'You're an absolute natural.'

'Maybe you should join ENSA,' Archie said. 'It wouldn't matter if you didn't have much experience. They don't earn the nickname Every Night Something Awful for nothing. You'd shine with that lot.'

'I can't see me doing that,' Bronwyn said. 'But when this war is over, perhaps I'll join an amateur dramatics group.'

We were interrupted by Thomas, the man who Bronwyn denied fancying. Although she tried to hide it, I saw her eyes light up as he approached her. He asked if she'd like to go for a drink.

'Don't worry about me,' I said. 'I'm heading off home now.'

I felt hopeful that Bronwyn might have found the right man for her. It had been a very long time since she'd had a serious relationship. Before we were posted to Bletchley, we both worked for the emergency services. For a while she was a motorbike courier and rode all round the country in all sorts of weather. She didn't quite have a bloke in every town, like sailors were supposed to have wives in every port, but she did have her fair share of boyfriends. Several of them were married. But things had changed. In those days, she certainly wasn't looking for any permanent relationship. Now, she thought differently.

Although she'd denied having feelings for Thomas for some time, I finally got her to talk about him. She owned up to some reservations. He was a widower with one daughter. We'd all grown up with fairy tales about wicked stepmothers and she didn't want to be disliked by his daughter. I tried to tell her she was jumping the gun. She hadn't really even had a date with Thomas much less discussed any long-term plans. And who was to know if his daughter would like her or not? They might eventually get on like a house on fire. Her experience with her younger brothers and sisters would stand her in good stead.

* * *

My boss, Helen, stopped at my desk, irritation showing in a rare frown. 'There's someone at the gate to see you.'

'Me? Here?' We weren't allowed visitors at the Park. The gatehouse man had a list of expected visitors, and didn't let anyone else in.

'He says he's your father. He's in uniform, apparently. Making a scene because he's not allowed in.'

'My father? Here?' I said like an idiot. I couldn't believe what she'd said. Bronwyn overheard the conversation and turned to me, her eyes wide.

I dithered. The last person I wanted to see was my father. He'd never been much of a dad. He always criticised everything I did and wasn't above giving my mum a backhander. She'd thrown him out when she found out he'd not only got another woman, but got her pregnant. I was there. Best day of my life.

'Well, you'd better go and see him,' Helen said. 'Send him away as quickly as you can. He's making a nuisance of himself, by all accounts.'

As I walked to the gatehouse, my mind ran over all the possible reasons why my father might come to see me. It was certain it wouldn't be anything good. I shivered and wished I'd stopped to put my coat on as I walked on the gravel path. The wind blew my hair about, and I pulled my cardigan tight, wishing I was anywhere but there at that moment.

As I neared the gatehouse, my mouth was dry and my shoulders felt under my ears.

There he was, looking for me, his big insincere smile plastered on his face. I knew that face so well, and had hoped never to see it again. I remembered a saying that you're born with the face God gives you, but by the time you're forty, you have the face you deserve. His face showed his selfish, cruel nature before he even opened his mouth.

To my amazement, he was in handcuffs.

The guard knew my face, but not my name. 'Are you Lily Baker?' he asked. I nodded and showed him my pass.

'This man says he's your father and must speak to you urgently. Are you willing to speak to him? I'm not letting him in. He's not on the list. You'll have to talk out here. I'll take his handcuffs off now I'm sure who he is.'

My heart sank. I'd have to speak to him, not that I wanted to. I confirmed he was my father, and the guard removed his handcuffs.

'I'll keep an eye on you in case he gets a bit overexcited,' he said, pulling a face.

'You're not in uniform!' were my father's first words. Trust him to criticise me as soon as he saw me, no *lovely to see you* from him.

'It's optional in some jobs,' I answered through gritted teeth.

'Is that trumped-up little Hitler serious about us talking out here? Out in the cold?' he said. He wasn't as cold as me. He was in army uniform and wore a greatcoat. But I was shocked at the change in him. He was still cocky and thought himself above everyone else, but he looked a lot older. More wrinkles, a slight stoop. He'd been very young when I was born, so he was only in middle age, but he'd aged more than ten years since I last saw him. That day when me and Mum threw him out. I smiled at the memory.

He misread my smile. 'Happy to see me, are you? Missed your old dad?'

My smile disappeared quicker than cakes at a kids' tea party. 'No. What do you want?'

'Who says I want something? I've just come to see my little girl.'

I glared at him, struggling to suppress rising anger. 'I'm a soldier, not your little girl. Now say what you want or sling your hook.'

A motorcyclist approached the gates, slowed down and was waved through.

'See that!' my dad said. 'Just sailed through. Could be anyone under that helmet. No handcuffs for him. Oh no!'

I knew that motorcycle messengers arrived at the Park all hours of the day or night, but I wasn't going to tell him that.

My shivering was getting worse and my teeth chattered. He stepped forward and tried to put his arm round me. 'Here, let me warm you up.'

I stepped back and knocked his arm away. 'I repeat, say what you want or bugger off. How do you know I work here, anyway?'

He raised his eyebrows. 'I'm good at finding you, me. Did it before when you moved to Sunbury. Remember? I tried to ask your mum, but she wouldn't tell me a thing. That old biddy next door, though, she was another matter. Said you were somewhere called Station X. Had no idea where the hell that was. It took me ages to find out. Anyway, this isn't the right place for a chat. I'll come to your place. What's the address?'

Breathless at his cheek, there was no way I wanted him coming to Happy Days.

I looked at my watch. 'I'll see you in the George and Dragon at seven o'clock.' At least there would be other people about. If he came to Happy Days, I might have to physically throw him out.

A spiteful look I recognised of old appeared on his face. 'But that's hours away. What'm I supposed to do till then?'

A church clock nearby struck the hour and reminded me that I'd be in trouble if I was away from work much longer.

'Go and hang yourself for all I care. Clear off!' I turned on my heel and went back to the guardhouse. I could hear him swearing as he stomped back down the drive.

'He's a right one,' said the guard. 'Seemed to think he was entitled to just walk in. Him a soldier and all. He should know better. They wouldn't let anyone just walk into his barracks, wherever they are.'

'I'm sorry you had to deal with him,' I said. 'He can be difficult.'

By now, we'd stepped into the guard hut, and I was relieved to be out of the cold wind. The hut smelled of paraffin and farts. 'Warm your hands on the heater, love,' he said and I huddled over the little circular paraffin heater that barely gave off any heat at all.

'You're not kidding. Your old man's difficult,' he said, looking up to heaven. 'I told him he couldn't come in because he wasn't on the list, and do you know what the cheeky bleeder did? He only snatched my list off me and wrote his name on it. "There, now I'm on it," he said. Must think I've come down with the last shower of rain. If that's your dad, I feel sorry for you.'

I wanted to hug him for his understanding and kindness, but needed to hurry back.

As I stepped into my hut, I took a few deep breaths, trying to calm myself. *It's okay, he's gone, I'm in control*, I said to myself and pushed my shoulders down.

'Everything okay?' Helen said as I walked back in.

'Fine, he's gone.' With that, I returned to my desk and put my headphones back on, wishing my heart would return to its normal speed. Bronwyn looked at me with a question in her eyes, and I mouthed, 'Tell you later.'

* * *

'I'll come with you!' Bronwyn said when I told her what had happened. 'Trust me, I've had to deal with a few rotters in my time. You must be tamping. You'll need me to help you keep calm.'

So at seven twenty we pushed our way into the George and Dragon. It was already busy and stank of beer and cigarette smoke. Old men were playing dominoes in a nearby corner; three old ladies, still wearing their coats and hats, sat next to the fire and I could hear a darts game in the other room. The faded red carpet was sticky, and the ceiling brown from decades of smoke.

'Is he here?' Bronwyn asked, looking around.

'He's probably got his arm round some girl,' I replied. Sure enough, I spotted him across the bar, trying to win round some girl who looked like she wanted to escape.

'Come on,' I said, and pulled Bronwyn with me. We wove our way through the drinkers and with each step I wished the evening were over. That instead we could be sitting in front of the fire at Happy Days reading, knitting or doing a jigsaw puzzle. Anything but here. With him.

At first he didn't see me, so I tapped the girl on the shoulder. 'You look like you want to get away from this bloke, but you're too polite to say so. Is that right?'

She nodded and scuttled off without a word.

He turned to me, fury in his eyes. Then I saw him catch himself, and the scowl was replaced with an insincere smile.

'Lil, you came!' he said, and attempted to kiss me on the cheek. I pulled away. He looked at Bronwyn. 'And who's your lovely friend? I always fancied a darkie myself!'

Bronwyn thought she'd have to keep me calm, but I thought she was going to hit him. If looks could kill, he'd have died on the spot. I put my hand on her arm. 'Take no notice of him. He's a moron.'

'Now,' I said, looking at him again. 'What do you want?'

'I want to buy you and your gorgeous friend a drink. That's what I want.' And before we could stop him, he headed to the bar.

Bronwyn was still trying to calm herself. 'I thought my old man was the limit, but I gotta say, yours takes the biscuit. Shall we throw the drinks in his face and leave? Or go now?'

I shook my head. 'I want to know what he wants first. Then we'll leave.'

He handed us each half a pint of shandy. 'Didn't push the boat out then,' Bronwyn said.

'How've you been, sweetheart?' he asked me.

I took a sip of my drink. 'This isn't a social conversation. What do you want?'

'To get to know you better. It's been a long time.'

I scoffed. 'Yeah, and you've missed me so much you've never written or tried any other way to get in touch.' I knew he'd written to Mum a couple of times trying to win her round. She'd just ripped up the letters and thrown them in the bin.

'Actually, there is something,' he began.

I recognised that wheedling tone. *Here it comes.* Now I find out what he wants.

'I wonder if you can do something for me,' he said, trying to smile again.

'Why should I?'

He touched my arm, and I pulled away. 'Maybe 'cos I'm your dad. I've always been good to you, haven't I?'

I had a mouthful of shandy and spluttered it all over him.

'That's not what Lily's told me,' Bronwyn said. 'Not joking or nothing, but you've been a right bastard to her and her mum.'

He turned on her so fast some of his pint spilled on the floor. 'You keep your black mouth shut!'

Rage showed in her eyes and, without hesitation, she threw her drink at him, glass and all. It fell to the floor and shattered, causing everyone nearby to look round.

He looked as if he could kill her, took a step forward, then thought better of it. Instead, he began brushing the beer off his coat, drops spreading over the floor round him.

'Come on, Bronwyn,' I said. 'We're leaving.'

But he blocked our path.

'It's just a small favour. I miss your mum...' I knew that meant he missed her cooking and having someone to bully.

'Will you ask her to take me back?' he went on. 'I'm being posted somewhere dangerous and...' I shoved him out of the way and he tripped backwards, knocking a drink out of another soldier's hand. The soldier looked at him in disbelief and started hurling abuse at him.

It gave us a perfect chance to escape.

It had got colder in the few minutes we'd been in the pub. 'It's nobbin' out here,' Bronwyn said. 'We'd better hurry back before we freeze solid.'

I put my hand on her arm. 'I'm sorry he was so rude to you. He's a nasty man.'

She shrugged. 'It's been a while since anyone called me a darkie...'

'But you're not. You just look like you've got a good tan.' In fact, I'd always envied that about her. My skin often looked pasty, especially in the winter.

'That doesn't matter to someone like your dad, does it? Anyway, I got my own back. His coat'll smell of beer for a good long time.' She paused. 'It's you I feel sorry for. Mind you, gotta say, I've never seen you like that. I was right impressed that you could be so chopsing. Good for you, girl. He deserved it.'

We heard footsteps behind us and spun round, but in the dark and blackout we couldn't see who it was. Bronwyn tugged at my arm and pulled me between two houses. She put her finger to her mouth, telling me to be quiet. The footsteps continued and went past. It wasn't him. Maybe he was still trying to sort out the soldier who was angry with him.

I hoped so.

6

'You look good, Carolyn,' I said. 'You've got much better dress sense than your boyfriend.'

She stopped admiring herself in the mirror. 'What do you mean? His dress sense is immaculate, if a bit formal.'

It was early evening, after a bright autumn day. We heard the clip-clop of a horse outside as it pulled its cart. 'Any old iron!' shouted the rag and bone man.

'He'll be lucky,' Carolyn said. 'The government's had all our metals. But what did you mean about George's dress sense?'

I wondered if I'd put my foot in it. She'd decided not to get involved with the panto because she wanted to go riding in her spare time. At home she had her own horse, but she'd tracked down a stable where she could rent one by the hour and was in her element. She was also meeting a lot of what she called 'our sort of people'. I wondered if she preferred to keep the two halves of her life as separate as possible because she said little about them.

Hadn't George told her he was going to be the pantomime

dame? Would she approve? Be embarrassed? Be annoyed he hadn't told her?

'Well, you know George is in the panto. He's got the main part, the dame Mother Goose. He's found a fantastic outfit for the first rehearsal. It got a lot of laughs without him having to say a word.'

She blinked and rubbed her neck. 'Dressed as Mother Goose?' her voice trailed off.

'That's right, he's going to be a star in the role.'

Before we said more, the doorbell rang. 'There he is!' she said, her voice slightly less excited than in the past. 'We're going out for a meal.'

She let him in and they both came into the living room as she fetched her coat and bag. Peggy was at work, but Bronwyn and I were there. He sat down with us, completely at ease. 'You were excellent as the magic fairy,' he said to Bronwyn. 'What outfit will you wear? Have you planned it yet? There is a lot of choice in the storeroom. I had fun picking mine.'

Carolyn came back in as they were discussing the pros and cons of wings or no wings, long fairy dress or short. 'I didn't know you were so interested in clothes,' she said, putting her hand on his shoulder.

He put his hand over hers. 'I always comment on what you wear, darling. For example, you haven't worn that beautiful dress since we went to the Barley Mow three weeks ago. The colour suits your hair perfectly. It makes you even more lovely than you are.'

I'd always admired Carolyn's dress sense and rarely saw her in the same outfit more than a few times. 'How come you have so many clothes, Carolyn?'

She smiled. 'When they announced that clothes would be rationed, Mummy and I went on a spending spree. We spent the day in London and had a simply wonderful time with tea at the Savoy. We had to get a taxi all the way home, we had so many boxes. I've had a couple of things altered by Mummy's dress-maker when I've been home though. I've lost weight with the awful food at the Park.'

'Gotta say what you did beats making do with jumble sale findings,' Bronwyn said, touching the fabric of Carolyn's black and white jacket.

'What about you, Lily?' George asked.

'Jumble sales for me, too, but I can sew. My mum showed me when I was quite young. I'm not above making a dress or a blouse out of a tablecloth or curtains if I like the look of it.'

Carolyn looked impressed. 'I had no idea you were quite so talented, Lily.'

'Bronwyn is too, with her knitting.'

She looked at the clock on the mantlepiece. 'Oh, good gracious, look at the time. We should be going, George.' She pulled him up. 'Have you remembered we're meeting a couple of my new riding friends? They're PLU.'

I frowned. 'What's PLU?'

'People Like Us. Our age, same background, country folk with money. We'll feel comfortable with them.'

Bronwyn and I managed to keep a straight face until they'd left. Then we had a fit of giggles.

'Poor dab,' Bronwyn said, 'having to put up with the rest of us. We're definitely not PLT.'

'What? What's PLT?'

She laughed. 'People Like Them. But fair's fair, she's always been nice to us, kind even, never treated us like we're beneath her, so I won't hold it against her. But seriously, if he is well... you know... he's got to be very careful or he'll end up in prison.'

'My mum always says it's a pity for their family. They'll never have kids and so no grandchildren. My dad, miserable sod that he is, always said it's disgusting. I call beating your wife disgusting, not that he'd agree with me or ever own up to it. Come to think of it, he thinks most things are disgusting or disgraceful.'

Bronwyn sighed and picked up her knitting again. 'Let's hope we're wrong about George. He's a lovely man.' She held up her knitting and measured it. 'Now, I think it's time to turn this heel. I always hate that bit. Tell you what, you're a dab hand with your old sewing machine. Why don't you make Linda a stocking to hang up for Christmas?'

My mind went to all my scraps of fabric and odds and ends of ribbon and thread. I loved a chance to play around with them, especially making something as simple as a Christmas stocking. It could have loads of fussy bits on it and no one would say it was too much. 'That's a great idea, but we don't know for sure if she'll be here.'

'No problem, is it? She can take it with her and her mum can fill it up.'

I wondered if her mum would have enough money for even modest Christmas presents. I decided I'd look on the Wanted and For Sale noticeboard near the canteen. Perhaps I could find some toys for her, or even some decent second-hand clothes. Her home looked short of everything and it would be good to send her home with more stuff than she came with. I just hoped Marion wouldn't see it as being patronising.

Mrs W. popped in, as she often did, and gave Linda an apple. 'Aintcha got a biscuit for me, then?' Linda asked.

'Not today, but an apple will be good for your teeth. An apple a day keeps the doctor away.'

Linda's eyes grew wide, and she grabbed hold of my hand. 'But my mum needs to see the doctor. We have to tell her not to eat apples.'

7

Only a few days after Dad came to the Park, I was concentrating on listening to messages from France when the boss signalled to me to stop. I took off my headphones, reluctant to stop halfway through a message. It was impossible to tell which ones might be of vital importance to the war effort.

'You need to go to the Hall, Lily,' she said. 'Room fourteen.'

I stood up and put on my coat. 'What's it for?' I asked. It was unusual to be interrupted when wearing headphones and making notes.

'I'm afraid I can't tell you. But it will all be explained.'

As I walked through the corridor, it smelled of furniture polish, something citrus like and calming. People walked here and there, some in uniform, some in civvies. All looked very determined, unlike me. My footsteps were hesitant with uncertainty.

I found the right room, knocked on the door, and was immediately let in by a lady in civvies. She was very elegant, wearing a tweed suit with a pink blouse underneath. She had an immaculate victory roll hairdo that I envied. I could never get that right.

She looked at me with sympathy in her eyes. I couldn't imagine why.

'Do sit down, Lily.' She indicated a chair on the other side of her desk. 'I'm Mrs Orson and it's my job to look after the welfare of staff here.'

I frowned and wondered why she'd need to look after my welfare. I hadn't been ill, or in trouble as far as I knew.

She went to a side table and poured me a glass of water, then sat down opposite. She leaned forward and held out her hand for mine. 'I'm afraid I've got some very bad news for you.'

My breath caught in my throat and my stomach dropped. It had to be Mum or Grant. Something terrible must have happened to one or the other of them. *Please*, I silently prayed. *Don't say something terrible has happened to either of them.*

'Is it my mother? Has something happened to her?'

She still held my hand, but shook her head. 'Your mother is fine. I just spoke to her on the phone. It's your father. He's had a heart attack. They rushed him to hospital, but there was nothing they could do. I'm very sorry, but I'm afraid he has passed away.'

I couldn't take in what she was saying and my hand went to my heart. 'He... Do you mean...'

'I'm afraid I do. Your father has passed away. He has died. Your mother telephoned and asked us to let you know. She would very much like you to go home and help her arrange the funeral.'

I felt breathless, disorientated. 'Um. Go home? Is that okay? Can I get leave?'

She pushed the glass of water towards me and waited until I'd taken a few sips. Then she passed a sheet of paper over the desk. 'I've arranged for you to have a few days' compassionate leave, and here is a travel warrant. It's probably too late now to head off, but you can go in the morning.' She looked at the clock on the wall. 'There's only about an hour of your shift left. I'll leave it to you if you want to go back to work. Your Head knows what's happened, and she'll understand if you want to go imme- diately.'

I left her office in a daze, went downstairs and sat on a chair in the corridor, trying to take in what she'd said. I put my head in my hands and tried to calm my breathing.

My father was dead.

It couldn't be true, I thought. I'd only seen him a few days before and he'd been fine. Even as I thought it, I knew that was an irrational thing to think, but I still somehow believed it. As if seeing him would magically keep him alive somehow. He was a horrible man, but he couldn't possibly be dead. He wasn't old enough to be dead.

Someone from my hut walked by. 'Are you okay, Lily? You look as if you've seen a ghost.'

I couldn't bring myself to talk about it, so I just said I was okay, but she didn't take me at my word and squatted down beside me.

'What is it Lily? Are you feeling poorly?'

I shook my head. 'No, it's not that. I... I just heard my dad died.'

She was kindness itself, and stayed with me until I'd calmed down.

'Please,' I said. 'I'll be okay now. It was just the shock. We weren't even close.'

'If you're sure. I'll tell Bronwyn. Her shift finishes soon. I'll tell her you're here, shall I?'

Maybe it was because I hadn't really taken in what I'd been told, but once the initial shock had passed, I couldn't work out how I felt about his death. Nonetheless, I kept running over the last time I saw him and was filled with guilt. That time at the guardhouse when I'd told him in no uncertain terms to get lost. Or go hang himself. Or later that evening in the pub, when I'd been rude to him and walked out when the other soldier was threatening him.

Had my words somehow caused his death? Was he so upset he'd overstrained his system somehow?

Would we ever really know what happened? Did something precipitate the heart attack? Had he been overworked? The army could be very reluctant to give out much information. But this wasn't a war death. He hadn't been somewhere fighting. He'd been stationed in England. It was only then I realised I didn't even know where he was stationed. Presumably Mum would have been told.

It was interesting that she must have been down as his next of kin. They had more or less split up when he joined up, and he'd been with someone else since. Perhaps he never got round to changing his next of kin details. I'd heard she'd thrown him out too, that would be why he was trying to get back with Mum. The other woman had a child with him, so presumably they'd been in touch for that reason. I wondered if he'd been paying her regularly. Knowing what he was like, he'd have done anything to get out of it.

I sat wringing my hands until Bronwyn arrived. She put her arms around me and hugged me tight. 'I heard what happened. I'm so sorry, *cariad*,' she said. 'Come on. Let's go to the Beer Hut, and I'll buy you a cuppa while we plan what you need to do next.'

Unusually, there were few people in the Beer Hut, and I was disappointed to find Peggy wasn't behind the bar. Then I remembered she was using her day off to be with Linda.

'Sit down by yere,' Bronwyn said, almost pushing me into a chair in the corner of the hut. 'I'll get the teas.'

She was back in no time with two teas and two pieces of cake.

'Tea and cake help with most things,' she said. 'Want to talk about it, *cariad*?'

I paused and stirred one spoon of sugar into my tea. 'It's weird. You know what he was like—'

'Well, let's say I didn't think he was a decent man,' she interrupted.

I was taken aback by her blunt comment, true though it was. But then I tried to think of good things he'd done. It was tough. He'd always worked, and always given mum her housekeeping. You couldn't say the same about all blokes. But if he ever found out she'd done any extra cleaning time for her ladies, he'd dock her money. I sighed.

'You're right. You saw what he was like in the pub the other night. I can't really think of good things he ever did. But it's still a shock. I almost feel like an orphan. Silly, 'cos I've got my mum.'

'What was he like when you were a little'n?' Bronwyn asked after she'd finished her mouthful of cake.

I tried to remember, but it was a struggle. 'Well, he was at work all day. Dads don't take much notice of their kids, do they?'

Bronwyn laughed. 'Wouldn't it be tidy to have a dad who did? Mine wouldn't have noticed if we'd hung upside down from the ceiling like bats when he came in.' She looked outside. 'It's dark already, let's get a bus back into town.' She put her arm through mine and we walked to the stop just outside the main gate.

At home, Peggy was playing with Linda, who had been at nursery all day. It was that time of day when children her age are tired and ratty, but you have to keep them awake or they'll have a little sleep, then be awake all evening. Peggy was doing her best to keep her amused playing Snap, but Linda was flagging.

When I told Peggy that my dad had died, she grinned. 'Well, no one's gonna miss him, are they?'

She wasn't wrong.

* * *

Dawn pushed its dim light round the edge of the blackout curtains in my bedroom as I turned off my alarm clock. I rubbed my bleary eyes and crept out of bed, trying not to wake Bronwyn. I shivered and thrust my arms into my dressing gown, picked up the clothes I was going to wear, then tiptoed into the bathroom. It was so cold in there, I could almost see my breath clouding in front of me. I checked the time and knew I had to get a move on to get the train I wanted. I got dressed and left my dressing gown on the back of the door.

No time for toast. I drank a glass of water and went out into the cold winter morning. The sun was just rising, softening the harsh outlines of buildings and bringing with it a flurry of activity. Early morning workers and shopkeepers hurried to their jobs, while others like me were heading for the station. My uniform shoes creaked with age as I hurried along Station Road. I'd sent Mum a telegram telling her I would be arriving and hoped it would put her mind at rest.

She knew better than to wait for me at the station. Trains were so disrupted because of the war, timetables became a wish list rather than reality.

Early morning golden light streamed between the platforms and dust motes danced in the glow. It was still cold enough to bite my face and fingers, and I thrust my hands into the pockets of my greatcoat.

'You work at the Park?' an elderly lady standing next to me asked. She'd have been alerted by my uniform. 'What do you do there?'

I smiled and pointed to a poster on the wall. 'Careless talk costs lives'. 'I just type boring letters,' I said. 'Where are you off to?' It was enough to take her mind off her questions, and she filled the whole time until my train arrived with stories of her family. I thought I could probably write a book about them. The toot-toot of the steam train alerted us to its approach and everyone on the platform came to life, preparing to fight for a seat.

The train was full, as always. Soldiers lined the corridors, sitting on kitbags, smoking, chatting, and trying to get off with any girl who walked by. Me included. I was lucky again and at the next stop someone got off and I grabbed a seat next to the window. The train slowed down, and I saw we were close to a farm. The farmhouse had ivy growing over it and the front door that had once been blue was sun faded to grey. Chickens scrabbled for insects nearby, and a noisy Scottie dog barked at them. They ignored him. The tall double doors to a barn nearby stood open, and a farmer was working inside on a tractor that had seen better days. It was a peaceful scene after the news of my dad and the stories the old lady had told me.

Ten minutes later, the train started up again. 'Wonder what the hold-up was this time?' someone in the carriage said to no one in particular. We were never told.

Pulling into Oxford station brought back memories of the first time I'd been there. After years of misery and abuse, Mum had worked out a way to escape my dad. She'd woken me up early one morning with the news she had a housekeeper's job in Oxford, and we'd be leaving behind everything we knew in Coventry. She'd already packed for me, and without even giving me time to have a wash, she dragged me out to the bus to the railway station.

I was familiar with Oxford station, using it each time I had leave. On Rowley Road, it had a sign over the entrance proclaiming 'London, Midland & Western Railway'. Just as happened that first time in Oxford, I crossed the road to the bus stops. But this time I had a kitbag, not a battered suitcase, and I wanted a bus to Sunbury, the suburb Mum now lived in and where I'd lived before I joined up.

'Sorry to 'ear about your dad, love,' our next-door neighbour, Edith, said as I hunted for my front door key. I just smiled and said hello.

The house smelled the same as always as I stepped inside. Vim, furniture polish and bleach vied for attention.

'Lily! You've come!' Mum said and rushed to hug me before I'd even put down my kitbag. I hugged her tight, remembering how much I'd missed her. She looked exactly the same – slim with wavy brown hair and a wraparound pinny over her dress.

'Come on, take off your stuff and I'll put the kettle on.' Tea was the answer to everything in our house – my dad being violent, not having enough money to eat anything but bread and marge, backache. Whatever it was, the kettle went on. It felt like home.

I'd managed to buy a few treats on my journey and put them on the table. She looked at them as if they were gold dust. The sausages were probably half full of sawdust and the tea would be mostly dust, but the tiny bar of chocolate was definitely worth having.

My coat hung up, I sat in my old familiar seat at the kitchen table. She spooned tea leaves into the brown teapot and pushed a piece of paper towards me. It was a telegram.

```
Deeply  regret  to  inform  you  that  your
husband Gerald Baker has died of a heart
attack today.
    Letter follows.
```

I turned it over, unable to believe that such dreadful news would be given so bluntly. There was nothing on the back.

'Got the letter just now,' Mum said as she put the knitted cosy on the pot. 'It won't be a military funeral because he wasn't killed in action, so I've got to bury him. Me! Bury the so-and-so.'

My jaw dropped open. Mum got a bit more money now. She worked in a factory, which paid more than cleaning, but she still lived hand to mouth. How on earth was she going to pay for a funeral?

'Do you belong to a funeral club?' I asked.

Her shoulders dropped. 'No such luck. Couldn't afford the sixpence a week. Anyway, you're young and I never expected to have to bury him. Why didn't his fancy woman get the telegram? That's what I'd like to know.'

'They fell out ages ago, didn't they? And she's got a little one to look after. I wonder if anyone's told her.'

She put the cups and saucers on the table, put the milk in a pretty jug, and poured the tea. 'How long can you stay?' she asked, a frown on her face. 'There's loads to do and I can't take much time off work.'

I put a little milk in my tea and stirred it. 'Up to a week, but they'd rather I didn't take all that time. We'll have to see how it goes. I don't suppose you've had time to do anything yet.'

A knock on the back door made us jump. 'Oh, it's Edith,' Mum said, opening the door to the neighbour I'd seen.

'Want a cup of tea, love?' she asked. Edith was a nosy gossip, but she had a heart of gold.

'Can't stop, pet, but I've got something for you.' She put a bag down on the table. There were coins rattling inside it. 'I had a whip-round of the neighbours, told them you had a funeral to pay for. Hope you don't mind. Anyway, they all gave you a bit, me too. It won't be much, not enough, but it'll help. Don't suppose you want a posh do anyway, do you? Not for him.'

Mum jumped up and hugged her. 'Edith, you are such a good friend. I can't tell you how much this will help. Me and Lily were just talking about the funeral. I've gone to the Co-op, they do a good funeral and I'll get loads of divi stamps. His body's being delivered there tomorrow.'

Edith put her hands on her hips, her mouth pinched. 'It's a disgrace, it is, them not paying for the lot. I know he didn't get killed in action, but even so, he was a soldier.'

'They do pay seven pounds ten shillings, but they take off the cost of the coffin and transporting his body. It won't leave a lot. They haven't told me if he had any money, but they're sending his stuff here. It should arrive tomorrow, the letter said.'

Edith headed for the back door. 'Let's hope his pockets are filled with five-pound notes. Don't hold your breath though, pet. I'm off now. Toodle-pip!'

We sat down again and had a second cup of tea. It was so watered down we could almost see through it. 'How're you feeling about Dad dying?' I asked.

Mum sipped her tea. 'I suppose I should feel something. We cared for each other once, a long, long time ago. It didn't last long, though. It was like once he got married, his true personality showed through.'

'So when are you working and what would you like me to do?'

She bit her lips. 'I've got to work tomorrow, but we don't have to be there when they deliver his body. I might have to work the next day, I'm not sure.' She went over to the kitchen drawer and took out a piece of paper. 'Here, I've made a list of things we need to do. Do you think we should have some sort of wake?'

I was surprised by the question. 'A wake? Who would we

invite? Who would want to come? It's only us and perhaps Edith, unless some of the people who worked with him want to come. Money's tight. I think you and me should just go out and have something to drink at the pub. We can have a drink to celebrate him being gone.'

She chuckled. 'Don't hold back how you feel, will you! You're right. No wake.'

She handed me the paper. 'Tomorrow, can you see how much of this you can get through? It'd be such a load off my mind.'

* * *

I'd never been to an undertaker's office before and I stood outside in the rain, huddled under a black umbrella, wondering what I had to do. The previous night, Mum and I had caught up on everyday news and avoided talking about Dad and his behaviour. We listened to *It's That Man Again* on the radio, glad to have something to make us laugh. But now she'd gone to work, and I was beginning the many tasks my dad's death had landed on us.

Taking a deep breath, I rang the bell and went into the Co-op office. I'm not sure what I expected, but it wasn't a homely woman who looked like everyone's granny sitting behind a desk and smiling. In front of her was a nameplate declaring she was Mrs Jane Thorpe. She was wearing a black suit with a white blouse underneath it.

There were two religious sayings in frames on the walls. *Blessed are those who mourn, for they will be comforted* and *For the Lord comforts his people and has compassion.* On the desk was a posy of holly and ivy.

Mrs Thorpe stood up, leaned forward and shook my hand. 'Good morning. How can I help you?' She indicated for me to sit down and I perched on the edge of the chair, feeling unsure of myself.

'My name's Lily Baker and my mother contacted you yesterday. My father died a couple of days ago. He was a soldier, and the army is delivering his body here today.'

She glanced at the big double-sided diary in front of her. Each page was edged in black. 'Oh, yes, I see we are expecting him. Are you here to arrange the funeral?' She got a notepad out of her desk. 'We have a list of questions we ask relatives. Is that okay?'

I nodded, and she picked up her pen. 'Full name and date of birth of the deceased?'

We went through all those factual points, then she put down her pen and looked at me. 'Now I need to ask you about your wishes for your father. I see a coffin is provided by the army. Do you wish to purchase a better quality one? We have a good range for you to choose from.'

I could just imagine what Mum would say if I agreed to that. 'No. The army one will be sufficient.'

She wrote that down. 'Now, there is a slot at the church in three days' time at four o'clock. Would that suit you and your family?'

'That will be fine. It will be a small turnout. My father didn't know many people.' And those he knew wouldn't want to come, I thought.

'Now, cars. Obviously, we'll provide a hearse to take the deceased to the church. I expect you'd like one for you and your mother as well. That's what people usually do.' She told me the price, and I went pale.

'No, thank you. We'll get a bus.'

She looked taken aback at that, but I wondered how most families afforded a funeral at all.

'We won't need a headstone either,' I said.

'But... families usually...'

'We won't need one,' I said firmly, and she scribbled on her notepad.

'Now, we will need to see the death certificate. If you haven't got it yet, your next task is to go to the registrar's office to get one.' She paused and looked at her book again. 'But in the circumstances, I believe the army doctor will have certified the death. In that case, the certificate will arrive with your father's body. Meanwhile, you should go to see the vicar to discuss what hymns and readings you would like. Reverend Boxley is who you need. He lives in the vicarage next to St Matthew's. Perhaps you can let me know if you or any of your family would like to view your father. We can arrange that if you give us a couple of hours' notice.'

I almost choked. I didn't want to see him alive, much less dead.

Leaving her office, I went to a café across the street and ordered myself a cup of tea. 'You bin to organise a funeral?' the waitress asked. 'Saw you coming out of the Co-op. Sorry for your loss. Was it someone close?'

'No, no one close,' I said, and to my relief she hurried off to serve someone else. Despite not feeling close to my dad, I felt a bit unsettled after organising the funeral. It made his death seem more real somehow. The sense of relief that I'd never have to see him again was still there, but so was sadness. Sadness that he was never the sort of dad I'd have liked. One who loved me and supported me in whatever I did. Played with me when I was a child, made me a doll's house, or took me to the park. But it was no good wishing the past was different. Mum had always made up for what he didn't do, and it was her who made me who I am.

A young mum with a little girl came into the café, and as I watched them, I remembered my dad's fancy woman had had a child. Mum wouldn't like it, but it only seemed fair to tell her the father of her child had died. Ages before, I had met her briefly. At that time, she was living with her mother. I had no idea if she still did, but guessed her mother would still be there and would know where she was.

My tea finished, I went to a phone box and called the army officer who had written to my mother. I put a penny in the box, pressed button A, and asked for him, but had to put in several more before they found him. My request was simple. Would any of the men who served with my father want to come to the funeral? There was a long pause and I heard the man clear his throat. 'I'm afraid that won't be possible. My men will be away for the next two weeks.'

Somehow, I doubted he was telling the truth. Was it that no one would want to come? I wondered. My dad never had many friends. He was too aggressive, too sure he was the one always in the right.

But it was another job ticked off my list.

My next phone call was to the vicarage. I was lucky, and the vicar was in and said he could spare me twenty minutes. I ran to catch a bus and was with him within half an hour.

He went through the obvious questions like name and date of birth, then asked what hymns I wanted. I hadn't a clue, so he suggested three. I told him two would be enough. We only wanted a short service and there would be very few people there. We settled on 'All Things Bright and Beautiful' and 'Abide With Me'. It felt hypocritical arranging all this. Dad was definitely an atheist, but there was no choice.

'And what reading would you like?' Reverend Boxley asked. I was tempted to say the shortest possible one, but didn't want to appear heartless. In the end, he suggested one I'd never heard of, and I agreed to it.

'So tell me about your father,' he said. 'I like to talk about the deceased.'

What could I say? He was a bad-tempered man who hit his wife and ran off with a younger woman?

I took a deep breath. 'He was a hard worker...'

He nodded. 'And?'

I shook my head. 'I'm very sorry, Vicar, but I can't think of anything else positive to say about him. He was a difficult man.'

He patted my arm. 'Please don't fret. He won't be the first difficult man I've buried. I have a way of wording the service that is tactful but honest. Leave it to me.'

I could have hugged him.

The bus stop was near the vicarage and I only had to wait for a few minutes for a bus that would take me near home. I queued for ages in the cold at the butcher's and managed to get a bit of beef. I'd make a stew and pad it out with some potatoes. I knew we had onions and carrots in the house and within half an hour of getting in from the cold, the house smelled wonderful. I found some flour and suet and made a jam pudding to steam on the top of the stew. It would all taste a whole lot better than the canteen at the Park. No cockroaches in it either.

The list of funeral tasks was nearly finished, but the most difficult one still remained.

Telling Dad's other woman.

* * *

Mum came in from her factory work, shivering with cold, her nose red and eyes watering. 'Bless your heart,' she said when she smelled the stew cooking. 'It's such a treat having someone cook for me. And you've lit the fire as well. You're an angel. How have you got on today?'

I made her sit down and served our stew into two bowls, along with two slices of bread. Bread got less recognisable every day the war went on. It was a horrible grey colour, and didn't taste much better than it looked.

She took a mouthful of stew and smiled. 'Mmm, that's lovely.'

'It's a lot better than the stew where I work. A girl found a mouse in her dinner one day! She screamed the place down.'

'I'm not surprised! Tell me again what you do. I'm never clear, and when anybody asks me, I'm not sure what to say.'

I gave her my well-rehearsed lie. 'It's just boring typing, Mum, dull as ditch water. Just letters mostly. You remember my friend Bronwyn? She works with me, so that makes it a lot better.'

She wiped her bread round the bowl, scooping up the last of the gravy. 'It seems silly to me to train you up in the army and then give you typing to do. Still, it sounds as if you're safe there and that's the main thing.'

We finished our jam pudding and a cup of tea, then it was time to tell her about my day. 'I've been to the Co-op. Dad should be there by now, and they think his death certificate will be with him. One less thing for us to do. The lady asked if we wanted to see him before the funeral.'

She sat back in her chair, folded her arms and then lit a Woodbine. 'You know, I think I do. If I see him there, in his coffin, I'll really believe that's the end of him. I'll never have to think about him, or worry about him knocking on the door, or knocking me about ever again.' She blew the cigarette smoke to the ceiling and waved it away with her hand. 'Will you come with me? I can finish early tomorrow if I tell them first thing.'

It was the last thing I wanted. Never seeing him again was fine with me, but I couldn't let her go on her own. 'Of course I'll come with you. Shall we say four o'clock? Meet you there?'

She nodded and blew a cigarette ring. 'Gosh, I can't do those very often. It must be a good sign.'

I began clearing up the dirty dishes, put them in the sink and put the kettle on again.

'I've been to see the vicar and chosen two hymns and a reading. I couldn't think of anything good to say about Dad, but he said he's used to that and has a special way of wording the sermon.'

'Pity we can't just drop him in a hole,' she said, stubbing out her fag. 'All this money for nothing. It'll only be us unless Edith comes, and I don't suppose she'll want to.'

I dreaded what I needed to say next. She wouldn't like it. 'That's the other thing I wanted to talk to you about. I think we should tell the woman he ran off with. They had a little one. They split up, I know, but she should still be told he's died. And her child might want to know when he gets older. I know you won't want to, but remember, she didn't know he was married. She didn't know he was two-timing you. He lied to you both.'

The corners of her mouth turned down, and her shoulders slumped. 'I suppose you're right, but I'm not going to tell her.'

So that was left to me the next day.

* * *

As I walked towards Grace's mother's house, I remembered the last time I was there. I was trying to find out where Grace lived because I knew she was seeing my father. So I pretended to be doing a survey. I never expected to actually meet her, or to find out she was quite pleasant and expecting a baby. My father's baby.

I wondered what had happened to her since then. She'd thrown Dad out. He told us that one time when he begged to come back to Mum. He never told us why, though, or what Grace was doing.

The front door at their home was faded blue, but the brass letterbox and key hole gleamed. The tiny front garden, barely big enough to be called that, was neat and tidy.

Getting in command of my nerves, I knocked on the door and took a step back. How would she react to the news? Would she be glad Dad had died or be sad? Maybe she loved him even if she threw him out.

Did she still live there?

I heard footsteps coming down the hall, and my stomach churned.

'It can't be Mummy,' I heard a woman say. 'She's got her own key. It must be a visitor.'

The door opened and there was Grace's mother. I'd met her last time, and she'd been kind, with no idea who I was or why I was there. She didn't recognise me. Like last time, she was wearing a wrap-around pinny over her clothes, a tweedy skirt and hand-knitted jumper.

I looked at the little child, a boy, the image of my father, and my breath caught.

'Can I help you?' she asked pleasantly.

'Is Grace in?' I struggled to get the words out.

She frowned. 'No, she's at work, won't be back for about ten minutes. What is it? Can I help?'

I had to think quick. Time was getting short before the funeral, so it was better to wait now even if it did mean telling this nice lady before I told Grace herself. 'Can I come in? I've got some news for her. Or if you'd rather, I'll wait out here.'

'Don't be daft. You'll freeze solid out there. Come in and I'll put the kettle on.' Holding the little boy's hand, she led me through the house.

'It's not bad news, is it?' she asked as she got out cups and saucers. She looked at the little boy. 'John, go and play with your train. I'll bring you a drink and a biscuit in a minute if you're good.'

At her invitation, I sat at the kitchen table. 'I'm afraid it is bad news. I don't know if you remember me, but I'm Lily Baker and Grace went out with my father.'

She stopped what she was doing and turned to face me. 'Him? That rotter? You're his daughter?'

I checked that the boy couldn't overhear what I was about to say. 'I'm afraid he's had a heart attack and passed away. Two days ago.'

She put her hand to her mouth and gasped. Then she sat down heavily on one of the other chairs. 'Dead? He's dead?' She frowned and shook her head. 'But he's not an old man.'

I reached out and put my hand on her arm. 'I'm afraid it's true.'

Before we had a chance to say more, the front door opened and Grace called out. 'I'm home, Mum!'

Her son heard her and rushed to greet her. She bent down and gave him a big hug and a kiss. 'How's my special boy been today, then?'

He just laughed and kissed her cheek.

'Grace!' her mother called. 'There's someone here to see you.'

She walked in, and I saw with surprise that she was a bus driver. Her uniform of trousers and a multi-pocketed jacket wouldn't have looked amiss in the military. She saw me and hesitated. 'Have we met before?'

'It's Lily, she's Gerald's daughter. She's got some bad news.'

Grace blinked several times and I could hear her breathing change. Without a word, she took her son into the living room and settled him with his toys. Then she came back into the kitchen and stood with her back to the sink. 'What is it?' she asked.

I couldn't read her expression.

'I'm afraid my father has passed away,' I said. 'I thought you'd want to know.'

She folded her arms and her jaw tightened. 'Let me guess. The husband of some married woman did for him.' The bitterness in her voice cut the air like a knife. Whatever my father did to her still hurt.

Her mother had returned to making the tea and got the milk from the cold cupboard. 'No, love, he had a heart attack. Not a day too soon, if you ask me. Let's have a nice cup of tea, while Lily tells you all about it. No good getting cross with her. She's just the messenger.'

Grace nodded, unfolded her arms and sat at the table. 'What happened then?'

I accepted the cup of tea her mother put in front of me. 'I don't know. Mum just had a telegram saying he'd died. Then next day she got a letter saying it was a heart attack. They've sent his body back. He's in the Co-op funeral parlour. I wanted to tell you in case you wanted to view him. They need a bit of notice if you do.'

She laughed. 'Of course not. I never wanted to see him again alive, much less dead.' She paused and looked from me to her son, who she could see through the kitchen door. 'So you're my lad's sister.'

'Half-sister,' her mum said.

'You don't look anything like my John.'

I shook my head. 'People say I look like my mum, not my dad.'

She put a spoon of sugar in her tea and stirred it before she spoke again. 'So what were the circumstances when he had the heart attack?'

'I don't know. The letter from the army didn't say. To be honest, now I've got over the shock, I'm just glad he's gone. He wasn't a good husband or father.'

Her mum sat down with us. 'Did you know him and my Grace had their wedding all planned? Never told us he was already married. Didn't care for anyone but himself, that's for sure.'

Although at the time I'd felt angry with Grace for going out with my dad, as soon as I learned he'd done the dirty on her, my feelings changed. She'd thrown him out and that must have taken some courage when she was in the family way. They could have got married bigamously. I'd heard loads of people got married a second time without a divorce because divorce was so expensive.

'He was always nice to me,' Grace said, tears in her eyes. 'Perhaps he wanted to do the decent thing.'

I fought the urge to tell her he'd been nice to my mum until they got married. There was no point in telling her, though. They hadn't married, and if she still had some happy memories, I wasn't going to ruin them.

'Do you want to go to the funeral? I think it'll just be me and Mum. You could all come. Mum would be okay about it.'

They looked at each other. 'No,' she said. 'We won't do that. Thank you for asking me.'

Her mum spoke quietly. 'You'll have to invent some story for your lad, Grace. Say he died heroically in battle or something.'

Grace bit her lip and nodded. 'Have you got a photo of him I could have?' she asked me. 'I tore mine up when I found out about him. It'd be nice for John to have one when he's old enough to start asking questions.'

Mum had torn up Dad's photos too, but I had one some-where. 'I'll send you one,' I said, pushing my chair back. 'I'd better go now. Mum's expecting me. Good luck for the future.'

As an unmarried mum, she'd need it.

* * *

'You've come to see Gerald Baker? Is that right?' the lady in the funeral parlour said. It was Mrs Thorpe again, the woman who I'd seen to arrange the funeral. She looked in her book. 'I see. Everything is in order. Can I just check who you are?'

Mum answered. 'I'm his wife and this is his daughter.'

'I'm very sorry for your loss, and I appreciate this is a difficult time for you. Sit down a minute, I'll check if everything is ready, and call you through. I should warn you, seeing someone who has passed on can be distressing. But Mr Baker will be in his coffin, and just look as if he's asleep.'

I looked around the room. It was clean and tidy, but the furni-ture looked like it belonged to the Victorian era, and it smelled like an old person's house.

She was back very soon. 'Come this way.'

We followed her down some gloomy corridors and I guessed one of the doors must lead to the main place where the bodies were kept. The corridor smelled of some sort of chemicals and the carpet was so thick we couldn't hear our footsteps. Turning to us, she stopped and showed us into a room. 'Take as long as you like. Ring the bell when you want to leave and I'll come and escort you back.'

The room was a modest size, perhaps twelve feet by fifteen. The walls were cream and on one wall there was a cream flowery curtain. A cross was on another wall. But the main item was the coffin, which rested on a table in the middle of the room. It was a simple one with brass-coloured handles on each side. I found I was holding my breath, just looking at it. I'd seen plenty of dead and dying people when I was an air raid warden but they were never anyone I knew.

I held Mum's hand as we walked towards it.

There, resting on what looked like pleated parachute silk, was the man who'd had such an influence on my life. He did indeed look asleep. In fact, he looked innocent, his face relaxed. He was never either.

'So, you're finally gone, you pig!' My mother's voice shattered the silence of the room. 'Not a moment too soon.'

Then she spat in his face.

I jumped back in surprise. I'd never known her to do anything like that, ever.

'Mum!' I said, my heart fluttering. Instinctively, I got out my hankie and moved to wipe away the spit.

'Don't you dare!' Mum hissed. She was still looking at him as if trying to keep the picture of him in his coffin in her mind forever. 'It's no more than he deserves, Lily. What I'd really like to do is kick him across the room!'

I stepped forward and put my arms round her. 'Come on, Mum, let's go.'

I pressed the bell for the lady to collect us and guided Mum to stand by the door.

'I haven't told you,' she said, 'but I made a change. He's having a paupers' funeral. He'll be buried in a grave with other people. No headstone, nothing. It's what he deserves.'

My heart went out to her. I couldn't argue with what she said, but I'd hoped that bitterness would have softened. I read somewhere that holding bitterness in your heart is like taking poison yourself and expecting the other person to die. It does them no harm, it just eats away at you.

* * *

'He's having a pauper's funeral?' Edith said. 'What'll people say?'

'I don't care what they say. That's my decision and I'm sticking to it. They do a very brief funeral.'

I remembered the planning I did with the vicar, but she assured me the Co-op would let him know. It might not even be him doing the service.

Edith didn't want to go to Dad's funeral. 'Sorry, love, but I'm busy that day, and you know I never cared for him much, anyway.'

It was a miserable day. A downpour had started the evening before and continued all night. The sound of the rain thundering on the roof kept me away for ages. We stood at the bus stop, huddling from the pouring rain. A clap of thunder made us both jump.

'Perfect weather for seeing him off,' Mum said, shaking her umbrella as the bus pulled up. Inside, it smelled of damp clothes and cigarette smoke. People muttered about the weather and rationing, a constant course of complaints.

As we drove through the rain-soaked streets, the sky darkened and there was a savage flash of lightning. I counted the seconds until the next boom of thunder. Five seconds. If it didn't stop, we'd be standing by the grave getting even wetter than we were. I hoped it wouldn't be near a tree or we risked getting struck by lightning.

We were the only mourners, and our footsteps echoed as we walked down the aisle of the chilly church and sat in the front pews near the coffin. There were no flowers, none even on the coffin, and no choir. The vicar, a different one, came and shook our hands. He was tall and reed thin. His trousers didn't quite reach his shoes, but his face was kind and his voice gentle. 'We'll just be singing one hymn and having one reading and a prayer. Then we will go to the graveside.'

I struggled to find my voice. 'Will he be buried on top of someone else?' I asked. I had no idea why that seemed important. After all, he would never know the difference. It seemed a final indignity, though.

The vicar clutched his Bible tighter. 'I'm afraid I'm never told that. The gravediggers will know. But I can tell you that his resting place will be recorded here in the church, so he won't be lost.'

We sang 'Abide With Me' and he read Psalm 23, 'The Lord Is My Shepherd'. I sat holding Mum's hand and felt it shaking slightly. Both our voices wobbled during the hymn, and she wiped her eyes during the reading. The whole time we were there, the storm strengthened, the wind howling like an injured animal. Its roar pounded on the windows and doors as if wanting admittance.

'Let's not go to the graveside,' she said. I was very relieved. It was a heart-wrenching event even in good weather.

We went to tell the vicar. 'I quite understand,' he said, his voice warm and empathetic. 'I'll do the usual brief reading even if there is no one there. May God bless you in your time of sorrow.'

The rain had eased just a little, and the storm was moving away. Mum looked at her watch. 'The pubs are open. Let's go and toast his burial.'

It was a pub we didn't know, which declared itself Paris inspired. It had several small round tables with a pair of chairs at each. Long windows across one wall were darkened by the inevitable bomb tapes, but it was still light and airy. 'Look, Mum,' I said, reading a board on the wall, 'they do cocktails. Shall we treat ourselves?'

She smiled. 'Never had one in my life, but why not? You choose one for me. Make a change from port and lemon.'

I had no idea what the cocktails were, so asked for two Martinis. 'Here's to freedom!' Mum said, holding hers up to clink mine. The Martinis were gone in a flash and next I ordered Singapore Slings. I felt sure I'd read about them in books. They sounded sophisticated. By the time we were halfway through those, we were both a bit light-headed and giggly.

'You know you were telling me about how Grant is a bit odd,' Mum said, struggling not to spill her drink.

'Not odd, just not recovered from his accident.'

She smiled. 'Whatever you say. I was thinking about him being a bit, what did you call it, distant? I've got an idea to bring him round.'

'Mmm,' I said, getting a taste of the pineapple in the drink. 'What's that then?'

She pulled me closer. 'Well, in my experience, limited though it is, the way to a man's heart is not in his stomach, like they say. Oh no, it's a few inches lower than that!'

My jaw dropped open. Mum never discussed such things. 'You mean I should...'

She pulled me closer still and whispered in my ear. 'That's right. Be like Mata Hari, seduce him. Got any sexy knickers?'

I choked and spluttered a mouthful of my drink across the table. 'Mum! What a thing to say to your daughter!'

'Well, have you? Got any?'

I went quiet. In fact, I'd been messing about with a spare bit of parachute material I'd found in a jumble sale and made a skimpy pair of knickers. Me and Bronwyn had a right laugh at them. They'd stayed in the bottom of my drawer ever since.

Was it possible Mum had had a good idea?

* * *

The next day was my last before I had to return to Bletchley. I planned to go to see some old friends and visit the picture house where I used to work. As I was gathering my things together, I spotted Dad's death certificate, which had been left on the table. I thought I might as well put it away with other certificates and important documents. I had no idea if we'd ever need it, but it made sense to keep it safe.

Mum had moved things around since I left, so I had to hunt for the old biscuit tin she used for the purpose. It was so old the picture on the front of a country cottage had almost faded away. I wondered if it had belonged to my grandmother. But I had a shock when I rifled through the papers inside. There, standing out from the certificates and other official papers, were three letters tied together with red ribbon. The post office stamp on the front said they were from Edinburgh in Scotland.

Letters to Mum from a man in Scotland.

I had no idea she knew anyone so far away.

Knowing I shouldn't, and feeling guilty, I nonetheless opened one. The address at the top was 37 Roberts Street, Leith, Edinburgh.

It was a love letter. The man, Percy, was saying how much he loved her, how he missed her, missed her body, and couldn't wait to see her. I felt myself blushing as I read it. No one likes to think of their parent having sex.

I dropped the letter and sat back, hardly breathing. My mum had had a lover. The letter wasn't dated and I couldn't make out the dates on any of the envelopes. Was this someone she knew before she met Dad, or after? Was a love affair her way of coping with a horrible husband? How on earth did she have a relationship with a man in Scotland?

Putting down the rest of the letters, I decided not to read more. They weren't mine, and I felt too uncomfortable with the knowledge they'd give me. I should never have read the first one and felt shame that I had. As I put them back in the tin, an old photo fell out. It was of a very attractive man, with dark hair and eyes and a smile anyone would fall for. I studied it closely. This must be Mum's man. On the reverse was the letter P, and a drawn heart.

I put it down and went to the bathroom. As I washed my hands, I tucked my hair behind my ears and, in the mirror, noticed the shape of my ears. They were slightly pixie like, a bit pointed at the top. Small ears that I'd always quite liked. My stomach clenched, and I went back to look at the photo. The man in the photo had exactly the same ears as me. It didn't prove anything, but left me with a lot of questions.

Mum had some explaining to do.

8

She was late coming home from work, and looked tired and cold as she walked in the door. 'Is that shepherd's pie I can smell?' she asked, taking off her coat and scarf.

I put the kettle on and laid the table. 'There's something I need to talk to you about, but it can wait until we've eaten.'

'Very mysterious,' she said with a smile. 'Are you still leaving in the morning? I hoped you'd stay longer. What with the funeral, and my work, I've hardly seen you.'

I put the beef stock in the saucepan and added flour to make gravy. 'I'm afraid so. Ten o'clock train, if it runs.'

After placing a cup of tea in front of her, I began dishing up the dinner. As always, the meal was more vegetables than anything else because they weren't rationed.

'How was your day?' she asked. 'Did you go to see your old boss at the picture house?'

We spent a few minutes talking about my old job and people we knew. By then we'd finished our shepherd's pie and I went upstairs. When I came down, she had moved into the living room where I'd lit the fire. 'Lovely and warm in here,' she said. 'It's freezing cold in that factory.'

Taking a deep breath, I put the love letters in front of her. 'I found these today while I was putting Dad's certificate away.'

It felt as if all the air was sucked out of the room. She went so still, I wondered if she was okay. I sat next to her and turned to face her. 'I've only read the top one. I stopped when I realised how private the letters were. I've seen the photo as well.'

Her breathing got fast and her face went puce. 'How dare you! Looking through my private stuff! You must have been really snooping.' She promptly burst into tears, and hesitantly, I put my arm around her.

'I'm sorry, Mum, I wasn't snooping. I was just looking for the folder where you keep important documents, so I could put Dad's certificate with them.'

She leaned back on the sofa, letting her hair fall over her face. She was trembling as she blew her nose and wiped away her tears. 'So you know...' Her words drifted away as she wept.

I hardly knew how to respond. I knew she'd had a relationship with a man called Percy, but that was all. I didn't know when, whether it was before or after she married my dad. I knew nothing about him or how and when the relationship ended. The letters looked old, so I guessed it wasn't carrying on now.

'I suppose it's none of my business,' I said at last.

She sobbed again. 'But it is. It is your business, more than you know.' She got up and poked the fire, putting on another lump of coal, avoiding my eye. A spark flew out and landed on the rag mat in front of the fender. She quickly stamped on it. 'I suppose I'd better tell you. I've tried to pluck up courage ever since me and your dad split up.'

I patted the sofa seat next to me. 'Come and tell me, Mum. But only if you want to.'

She sat down and picked up the photo of Percy, stroking it with her thumb as she gazed at it. 'It was in Coventry. Me and your dad worked in the same place, and Percy had a butcher's shop a couple of doors along. I used to pop in on my way home from work for something for tea. I wasn't going out with your dad then, but he kept asking me. He was dead keen.'

'So, you had two men after you?' I asked.

She nodded and put down the photo. 'Your dad knew Percy was interested and, like always, he had to win at everything. But he didn't win me at first.'

'But Percy wrote to you from Scotland.'

'He'd gone to look after his mum. She was very ill, and she died when he was there. Or that's what he said.'

There was a loud scratching at the back door and she stood up. 'That'll be Misty, Edith's cat. She often pops in in the evening if Edith's out. Likes a bit of company.' She let the cat in, put the scrapings of the dinner on a saucer for her and then let her into the living room with us. She was a beautiful cat, grey with long hair and a purr that sounded like a steam train. As soon as Mum sat down, Misty jumped onto her lap, and Mum stroked her and tickled her ears.

'You were saying Percy went to Scotland?'

'I've never wanted to go to Scotland since then. Never been, never will.' She rubbed her face with her hands, and Misty's purr got quieter.

'Why not? Did something happen while he was in Scotland?' I couldn't imagine what could happen while he was tending an elderly relative.

'I didn't know it, but he had a childhood sweetheart there. He'd lived there a few years before for a while. They'd always kept in touch, writing regularly. And he aways had his holidays there. Well...' She sobbed again and wiped her eyes. 'While he was there, he married her. If you'd have kept reading, you'd have seen the last letter was telling me all about it. I'm so sorry. I should have told you I was more or less engaged.'

'So you'd actually been going out with him?'

She nodded again. 'Only a few times, but we got close really quickly, if you know what I mean.'

I could guess and didn't want any further information in that respect.

She paused for ages and I thought maybe she wouldn't tell me the rest of the story, but eventually she straightened her back. Again, she spoke without looking at me. 'By the time I got his letter, I was a couple of weeks late. I've always wondered if he'd have come back and married me if he hadn't already got someone up there.'

I licked my lips. 'So...' I didn't dare ask what I wanted to ask. I'd seen the dates on Mum and Dad's marriage certificate and long ago worked out she was in the club when they got married.

She leaned over and took my hand. 'I'm so ashamed of myself. I should never have done it. Please forgive me.'

'But...' I was puzzled about where this story was going.

'I was worried sick. I knew your gran and grandad would throw me out if they found out I was having a baby. My friends said I should have it adopted. That would have been you, of course. I just couldn't do it. I couldn't give away Percy's child, even if he had turned out to be a rotter. I was still in love with him, silly thing that I was. Life would be a lot easier if we could turn off love like a tap.'

She put the cat on my lap and stood up. 'I've got a couple more photos you'd be interested in.'

A few minutes later, she was back. One photo showed Percy with his arm around her, smiling at the camera. They looked so perfect together, so happy. The other photo was him outside a butcher's shop. *Watson & Son*, it said over the window. He was wearing a butcher's apron and holding what looked like a pack of sausages. Again, that devastating smile.

'He was a good-looking man,' I said, handing the photos back to her.

She looked from the photos to me. 'That's where you get your good looks from.'

What she'd said up until then already told me he was my father, but her saying it so bluntly caused a sudden coldness that reached my very core. The news finally sunk in. My thoughts became fuzzy, and I tried to take in all the implications of what she'd just said.

I'd been lied to all my life.

My horrible father wasn't my father.

If my mum had lied to me about this, what else had she lied about? Did my 'dad' know? Was that why he was so horrible to me all my life? A hundred questions went through my mind. How? When? Why?

I needed time to absorb all this. 'I'm going for a walk,' I said. As I put my coat on she followed me into the hall.

'Please, Lil, don't hate me. I just did what I thought was best. It was the only way I could keep you.' Her voice was desperate, pleading.

'We'll talk about it some more when I get back,' I said.

Outside, I took my shielded torch out of my pocket and headed for the main road. Once an eight-foot wall had separated our corporation houses from the posher houses nearer the shops and bus stops. But that was gone, and in the dark it was impossible to tell any difference between them. It had rained earlier – the streets were slick and the feeble light from my torch reflected on them. Clouds moved quickly across the sky, exposing then hiding the moon and stars.

As I walked, my mind was still foggy. Although I didn't consciously think about what my mother had told me, I trusted somehow I would make sense of it at some time. But maybe not today. I thought of Grant having to absorb his life-changing injury, losing half his leg. His loss was so much greater than finding your father wasn't who you thought he was. I wasn't who I thought I was. Even so, my experience helped me to understand Grant's behaviour a little more.

The clip-clop of a horse's shoes brought me round from my muddled thoughts. The driver of the cart doffed his cap. 'Cold night for a walk!' he shouted. It was, and his comment made me realise I was shivering, but I was still not ready to go back. Instead, I did something I'd never done in my life before. I went into a pub on my own. Women rarely did that, and I was sure Mum never had.

Two older women looked up as I entered and seemed to wait for a second person – someone to come in with me. When they saw I was alone, they went back to their talk, their knitting needles moving without them giving them any attention.

I was pleased to see it was a woman serving. 'What can I get you, love?' she said with a smile. 'Come in to get out of the cold?'

'Something like that. Half of shandy, please.'

'I don't think I've seen you round here before,' she said as she checked my glass and poured my drink. 'Do you live around here?'

'I'm in the army, based at Station X. I've come home to see my mum.'

'Station X?' A man standing next to me said, with a sneer. 'No such place. You must think we came down with the last shower of rain.' He turned to the barmaid. 'She's having you on.'

Calling Bletchley Park Station X always led to these difficult conversations. I couldn't be bothered to argue with the man. It would have been a waste of time, anyway. His sort always knew everything. They especially knew more than any female they'd ever come across.

As I looked for a seat, the two women near the fire called to me. 'Come over here, love,' one said. 'The fire'll warm you up. You look ready to drop.'

I was grateful to join them, not just for the heat, but also for the conversation to take my mind off what I'd just learned.

'So, you're in the army, then,' one said, still knitting.

I nodded. 'Yes, but I only do boring office work. Nothing exciting to tell you, I'm afraid.'

Disappointed, their talk turned to who had got a new grandchild, who was carrying on with someone other than their husband while he was away fighting, and the shortage of eggs.

Their voices drifted over me as the fire lulled me into a drowsy state. I may not have cared for the man I'd believed was my father, but his death and organising his funeral had taken it out of me. And my mother's news still seemed unbelievable.

'You okay, love?' the lady with the hat like a tea cosy said, nudging me. 'You looked about ready to slide off that seat onto the floor.'

'I'm okay. Just had a very busy few days. And I'm back to work in the morning.'

Although I couldn't talk about my work, they were keen to know where I was living, what I did in my spare time, and anything else they could winkle out of me. 'I think I should get you another shandy,' the tea cosy lady said when they paused for breath.

'No thanks,' I said, standing to put my coat and hat back on. Only then did I notice I'd forgotten my gas mask. I saw they both had theirs at their feet. 'It's been lovely talking to you both. I'd better be off now. My mum will think I've got lost.'

Or maybe she would hope I had.

* * *

I'd barely stepped inside the front door when Mum was in the hall waiting for me, an anxious frown on her forehead. 'Are you okay, love?' she asked, trying to help me take off my coat. 'You've been a long time, you must be frozen.'

I took her arm and led her back into the living room. 'I popped into the Bell and Whistle and had a half of shandy. Two old ladies found me a seat by the fire and chatted to me non-stop.'

'As long as you're okay,' she said. 'There's a bit of sherry left over from last Christmas. Shall we have a drop?'

Getting out the cheap sherry glasses, struggling to take the cork out of the top and pouring the drink was an ideal distraction from our conversation.

We sat down again by the fire. 'Do you want to tell me the rest of the story, Mum? Is it too much for you? You looked so upset earlier.'

She took a sip of her sherry and pulled a face. 'I've got to tell you now. I can't let you go back tomorrow with only half the story. I worry what you'll think of me. We've always been so close.'

I put my hand on her arm. 'We still are, Mum.' I thought about what the woman in the pub were talking about – women who were carrying on while their husbands were away. If I spent my life thinking everyone had to behave perfectly I'd have a miserable time. It wasn't even as if I'd been perfect myself.

'Go on, what happened when you found you were in the family way?'

'I was frantic. Being sick in the mornings and trying not to let my mum and dad notice. Worried she'd spot I hadn't had my monthly. And heartbroken at being dumped by Percy. I thought me and him would be together for ever. What a fool, I was.'

Her story made me think of Peggy. It might be over twenty years after Mum's experience, but people were still harsh to girls who got pregnant without being married.

'So, how come you ended up marrying Dad?' I couldn't get used to the idea I'd have to call him something else. Or perhaps I wouldn't.

'I told you he'd always wanted me. I knew he wasn't a great catch but I was desperate, frantic. I let him know I'd go out with him. Even on our first date he wanted to go all the way. Proper pushy he was.'

'Sounds like him, all right.'

Misty, who'd sat on her knee again, got up, stretched and headed for the back door. 'Time to let her out,' Mum said, getting up.

'Now where was I?' she said when she sat down again. 'Oh yes. You'll think I was dreadful but I told your dad he couldn't... you know... unless we was married. He'd had more than a few drinks and he promptly fell on one knee and proposed. To be honest I'm sure he didn't realise what he was doing. He thought it was a joke.'

My jaw kept dropping open as I listened. 'Wow, you were so cunning. What a schemer you are.'

Her mouth turned down. 'I lived to regret it, of course, but if I hadn't been scheming I'd never have you. Anyway, next day I think he'd more or less forgotten he'd proposed. Had a thick head too. But I went round telling everyone at work we was engaged and they kept congratulating him. He'd have looked a fool if he'd backed out then. Anyway, he still wanted to...'

'So he went along with it,' I said with a sigh. What a mess, I thought, remembering the years of misery she'd suffered with him.

'I didn't give him much choice. I went and got the banns read next day and we got married three weeks later.'

My sherry glass was empty so I topped both of our glasses up. 'But didn't he realise that the dates were wrong?'

She laughed. 'Oldest trick in the book. Early baby. Men never know different anyway. I nearly came a cropper just after you were born though. They didn't let your dad in while I was in labour, of course, but when the midwife came out after I'd had you he overheard her talking to another nurse. "Early baby, my eye," she said, "eight and a half pounds!"'

'You always said I was a big baby.'

'You were, and it nearly gave the game away. He didn't really know, but after that your dad was always suspicious. Never wanted to let me out of his sight. Well, you know all about that.'

I tried to imagine being that desperate, being willing to marry a man you didn't think that much of. How hard times were for women. The war was definitely making it better because women were doing a lot of jobs only men had done in the past. But there was no way we were equal yet. Not by a long way.

'So did Percy stay in Scotland?'

She sighed. 'No, he came back to Coventry, back to working in the butcher's with his dad. I used to go to any butcher's but his. It was too painful to see him and his wife. She worked there, too.'

'Gosh, that must have been hard. Did Dad ever say anything about him?'

'No, but sometimes I'd see him looking at you in a funny way when you was a nipper, and I thought he was trying to see if you looked like him, or Percy.'

I got up to put a small lump of coal on the fire again. No use putting more because we'd be going to bed before long. 'So all these years you've kept this secret. It's not long since we left Coventry. Did you keep tabs on what happened to Percy?'

She looked down at her hands. 'No, I avoided anywhere where we'd been together and most people I knew didn't know him. I suppose he's still there, in the butcher's. With his wife.' She yawned. 'That sherry's made me sleepy. I'll go to bed now, love. I'm sorry to have told you all this when you're leaving tomorrow. It's a lot to take in. Hope you manage to sleep well.'

The bedroom was so chilly I put an old jumper on over my pyjamas and jumped into bed as fast as I could, pulling the blankets up to my nose.

So my real father still worked in a butcher's shop in Coventry. Maybe I'd go to see him.

* * *

'WHAT! So that miserable old you-know-what's not your real dad? Gotta say, that's a turn up for the books.'

I'd grabbed Bronwyn at the first opportunity when I got back from Mum's to tell her the news. Not that I'd completely taken it in myself yet.

'And your mum tricked him into marrying her? Can't blame her, but she paid a heavy price, poor dab. Putting up with him all those years.' She paused. 'Do you think he guessed, and that's why he was so horrible to you?'

I shrugged. 'Who can tell? He was miserable with everyone, except when he wanted something. Then he could be as nice as pie.'

'You said you've got a photo of this Percy. Let's be having a look.'

She took the photo from me, looked at it closely, and let out a little whistle. 'Well, if your dad ever saw this Percy, and according to your mum, he did, he couldn't help see how much you look like him.'

We were having our break at work and getting some fresh air after sitting at a desk for hours. I stretched my back, and it seemed like my spine creaked with the movement. It was a typical December day, dank and dreary. The trees that had leaves all year drooped as if they were sad, and even the birds were silent.

'Come on, let's walk quick, or we'll never get warm again. Those huts are always cold.' There was a thin skin of ice on the lake and a couple of brave ducks were sliding across it. A dog barked in the distance and a motorbike messenger arrived and went to the side door of the big house.

After a quick circuit of the lake, we headed to the canteen to get a cuppa to warm up.

'Do you want to see this Percy? Your real dad?' Bronwyn said as we waited to get our cup of dark brown liquid that could barely be recognised as tea. 'I'd want to if it was me.'

I nodded. 'I've thought about it a lot. I want to see him, but I don't think I want him to know who I am. After all, he doesn't know I exist. He might be horrified, especially if his wife doesn't know he was two-timing her.'

'So just see him, is it? Have a peek, maybe say hello? Incognito. Like a spy? It sounds fun. Trouble is, how on earth would you find him?'

'He's a butcher, Mum said, and in another photo she showed me he was standing in front of a butcher's shop – Watson's Butchers it was. There can't be many of them in Coventry with that name. It's probably the only one.'

We gulped our tea and began walked back to our hut. 'We're both off tomorrow,' Bronwyn said. 'Fancy a day trip to Coventry?'

* * *

'Was this station bombed, then?' Bronwyn asked as the train pulled into Coventry. 'It looks okay.'

I put on my coat and hat. 'It was. The bombers made a right mess of it. Operation Sonata, the Nazis called it. It's a couple of years ago now, but I remember reading about it.'

A woman standing next to us, waiting to get off, overheard our conversation. 'Hundreds died, they did, me ducks. Right fire-ball in the town centre, and do you know, a tram was blown right over a house. Landed in someone's back garden without its windows even broken.'

We said goodbye to her and headed to the bus stop outside the station. 'Before we look for the butcher's, I'd like to have a quick visit to where I used to live.'

'Was that near where the butcher's is?' Bronwyn asked.

'No, but we can get buses. We've got all day. Now, look for a bus to Willenhall.'

We stood for twenty minutes in the cold waiting for the wretched bus. 'The buses have never been the same since the bombing,' an elderly man told us. He looked poverty thin and didn't have a single tooth. 'The council've done some rebuilding, but a lot of buses had to change their routes. The town centre was flattened; market, cathedral, Daimler works, the lot. They said that King George cried when he saw what was left of the cathedral. Blarting like a kid he was, they said.'

'That's crying,' I whispered to Bronwyn, seeing her bemused expression.

The bus went near enough to the town centre for us to see how much destruction still existed. Looking at the fallen stones, burned walls and bomb craters made my stomach contract as I remembered my time with the ARP. Especially the day when I was caught by a bomb blast and knocked unconscious.

Coming back to the moment, I saw a building I recognised. 'Not far now,' I said and pressed the stop bell.

Bronwyn looked around as we got off the bus. 'Not being funny or nothing, but this looks like a right rough bit of town.'

The buildings were shabby before the war and were shabbier now. Broken fences and paving slabs, dog dirt on the pavements, years old posters on walls. Despite the cold, kids were playing out in the streets, most of them without a warm coat. They had red, runny noses they wiped on their sleeves. A mum was pushing her baby in a pram that was old enough to have belonged to her grandmother. Two older women leaned over a low wall dividing their houses and gossiped.

'Do you know,' I said, looking around with a fresh pair of eyes, 'I never really noticed it when I lived here. It was just normal for me. Me, Mum and Dad lived in two rooms round the corner. Shared the bathroom with two other families. I'll show you. Better keep a tight hold on your purse.'

Bronwyn grinned. 'Here's me saying this area is rough. Where I lived in Swansea was ten times worse. Ten families had to share one toilet in the garden. The smell! Half the time, the blokes didn't wait and went anywhere, especially when they were drunk. You had to be careful where you walked, I can tell you. Buzzing, it was.'

We went round the corner and there was my old home. Three storeys high, shabby front door and weeds in the apology for a front garden. As we stood outside, I was amazed to see our old neighbour walk past. I couldn't remember her name, but I remember she had a poison tongue. I looked the other way so she wouldn't recognise me, even though I was in uniform and it was several years since she'd seen me.

'I've seen enough,' I said, tugging at Bronwyn's arm. 'There's a library not far away. They should have a trade directory. We can look up the address of the butcher's. Mum never told me where it was.'

No one would have called the library warm, but it felt like heaven after being outside in the bitter wind. The librarian handed me the directory. 'It's a few years old, I'm afraid, but it's the most recent one I have.'

The directory was in two sections. One was addresses and the names of people who lived there, the other was businesses. They were alphabetical, so it didn't take me long to find Watson & Son. Churchill Street. The librarian kindly showed us on a map where it was and told us which number bus to get. Half an hour later, we were standing in front of a butcher's shop in Churchill Street.

It wasn't Watson & Son.

We stood looking at it, not believing our eyes. Had the directory been wrong, or had it changed hands?

'Perhaps he decided to change the name,' Bronwyn said. 'We should go in and find out.'

I felt as if all the air had been punched out of my lungs and I held on to Bronwyn's arm for moral support. 'There's a café a couple of doors down. Let's go in there first.'

It was lunchtime, and the cafe smelled of egg, bacon, and chips. The smell warmed us up almost as much as being out of the wind. We ordered two bacon butties and tea and sat down near the window.

'You're not going to chicken out now, are you?' Bronwyn said. 'We've come all this way in the cold.'

I held my cup with both hands, trying to warm them up. Truth was I wanted to run and hide and my insides felt wobbly. I knew I was being stupid. I was in no sort of danger, and the fact that the name had changed meant Percy, my real father, probably wasn't even there. As the waitress brought our sandwiches, she smiled. 'Haven't seen you before, me ducks. You just visiting or thinking of moving here?'

'I was hoping to go to the butcher's, Watson and Son, just down there, but it seems to have changed hands. Do you know what happened?'

She wiped her hands on her apron. 'I've only been here a couple of months, but I heard someone say they had some bad luck and moved the business across town. Chapelfields, I think they said.'

My heart sank. Another bus trip in the cold. I hoped it wouldn't be another wild goose chase.

Bronwyn had been listening. 'I'm not going to lie,' Bronwyn said, wiping bacon grease off her chin. 'That's disappointing. But we've come all this way, so we might as well go there. You'll owe me a shandy after, or two or three.'

Someone had left a newspaper at the next table and I picked it up. 'Rommel's tanks retreat in the north,' it said.

'I don't know about you, Bronwyn, but I have trouble keeping all the theatres of war in my head. Bad enough with what we...'

I stopped speaking because there were people nearby.

'I do, too,' she said, covering for my almost mistake. 'We seem to have been at war forever.'

'The last one lasted longer,' an old man at the next table said. 'Let's hope this one doesn't last four years as well.'

We finished our sandwich and went back to the bus stop.

* * *

There was only one butcher's shop in Chapelfields and it wasn't Watson & Sons. We stood huddled under our umbrellas and groaned.

'It looks like we're on a fool's errand, *cariad*,' Bronwyn said. 'But we may as well go in and ask if they know anything.'

A mum was buying a tiny portion of scrag end of neck as we went in, served by a young man, perhaps a year or two younger than me. We waited patiently, looking around at the spotless shop. A lot of the window display was taken up with paper rosettes, no doubt put there to hide the lack of meat on offer. There were signs on the walls about how much meat each person could have, and how many coupons were needed.

We waited until it was our turn and then I stepped forward.

The young man took one look at me and the blood drained out of his face. He staggered and grasped the edge of the display to keep himself upright.

Bronwyn and I looked at each other, baffled. He looked as if he'd seen a ghost.

It took him several seconds to compose himself. Then he shook his head and spoke. 'I'm so sorry. You look so much like my late sister, I thought I was seeing a spirit.'

My mind went into overdrive. Did I look like his sister? His dead sister? It wasn't impossible if we had the same father. But everyone always said I looked like Mum. And this wasn't Watson & Sons.

I didn't know how to reply to his comment, so I just asked if he knew where Watson & Son's butchers were.

His shoulders slumped. 'They closed down, I'm afraid. I'm James Watson.'

I had to think quick. I didn't have a cover story. I thought I'd just go into the butcher's, see my father, buy something and leave. I only wanted to see him.

'So you're working here now for someone else?' Bronwyn said. She was thinking quicker than me.

He nodded, and a tear came to his eye. 'Yes, my father was

killed in the bombings two years ago. And so was my sister. The one who looked just like you.' That last comment was aimed at me.

Poor man, losing his father and sister like that.

'Is there anything I can help you with?' he asked. 'We've got some lovely tripe left.'

I forced my mouth into a smile. 'We'll leave it, thanks. Sorry to have bothered you.'

It seemed I was never going to meet my real father after all.

As we walked away, Bronwyn asked, 'Aren't you going to tell him who you are? You're his half-sister, it might be a comfort for him to get to know you.'

I stopped in my tracks. 'You're right. The trouble is, if I tell him who I am, I'll be telling him his father made my mother pregnant while he was engaged to his mother. I don't want to spoil his memory of his father.'

She gave a low whistle. 'You're right, *cariad*. I hadn't thought that through. It might help him to have a half-sister, but it might be another blow when he's already had enough grieving. It's best left alone.'

I felt sorry not to get to know my half-brother, it would have been good to do so. But that was what I wanted. It wasn't what he needed.

9

It was my day for an 8 a.m. to 4 p.m. shift. I woke at six thirty, warm under my pile of blankets, but my face was cold. Even for early December, the day promised to be gloomy. It was still dark and likely to be for a while yet. Reluctantly, I threw back the covers and hurriedly put on my dressing gown, tying it tight round my pyjamas. Trying not to disturb Bronwyn, I opened the curtains just a little to see if it was raining. But the windows had a thin coating of ice on the inside, and I had to scrape a square off with my fingernail to see outside. No rain.

I tiptoed to the bathroom and had what my mum called a lick and a promise wash. The water and the room were far too cold for anything else. After creeping downstairs and making myself some tea and toast, I headed out of the door wearing my great coat over my uniform, two scarves, a pair of gloves and mittens over them. I tried to cycle to work whenever possible – it saved the bus fare, and I needed the exercise because my work was sitting down all day – but this day I decided to get the bus to avoid getting frozen.

As I stood shivering at the bus stop, I thought about my plan to visit Grant after work. I hadn't warned him for fear he would tell me not to come. A dog trotted by and looked and me and the other passengers waiting in hope. It was a skinny animal with big sad eyes that pleaded for food. I reached into my bag and tore a bit off half of the sandwich I'd made for my mid-morning snack. The dog swallowed it in one go, and looked at me beseechingly again. I shook my head and patted him.

'You'll never get rid of him now,' another passenger said. 'He's here every morning, regular as clockwork.'

I was glad the bus came along so I didn't have to look at the poor thing any longer, and as I settled into my seat, my thoughts returned to Grant. I'd been told he'd moved into his flat two days earlier and I'd put a letter through his door, so he must have got it. No response. Should I tell him about my plan for the veterans' show or would that guarantee he wouldn't turn up? I had to find a way to trick him into coming and resolved to talk to Archie about it. Carolyn had been as good as her word, and within a couple of days had most of the organisation for the show done.

My work was, as usual, decoding messages about events in France, resistance activities, demands for more resources, news of deaths and capture.

I'd been listening to the radio operator when the message was suddenly cut off mid-stream. I spoke to my supervisor about it, wondering what had happened.

'It's sad, but she was probably found by the Nazis. The average life expectancy of radio operators once they start is only three weeks.'

My jaw dropped open. 'Three weeks! That's dreadful. Do they know that when they take on the job?'

She nodded, her eyes sad. 'They do. They're absolute heroes. When they're captured, they're tortured to give up the names of the people in their cell. Their orders are to try not to disclose anything for at least forty-eight hours.'

'To give the others time to get away?' I asked.

'That's right. The poor things have to keep moving. They can't use the same place very often to transmit because the Germans will track them down.'

I tried to imagine their lives. Living in fear of every noise, every movement, every day. Moving from place to place, never having anywhere to call home, living out of suitcases, the taste of dread in their mouths all the time. I thought I'd never be brave enough to do what they did.

'Most of them are women, you know,' she said. 'If they walk around with a bag, people just assume it's shopping, not a radio. But enough of that. I've probably said more than I should. Go and have your break now, and try to put it out of your mind.'

Taking what remained of my sandwich, I headed to the big house. Winter had painted the buildings and the grounds in colours of brown and grey that matched the heavy clouds overhead. The bright autumn leaves I'd enjoyed kicking a few weeks before were gone or turned to mush underfoot. A strong gust of wind pushed against my face, throwing my hair around as I struggled the few yards from my hut.

Usually, I'd head straight to the canteen to find someone to chat to and a cup of tea. But I was on a mission. I needed to find Archie, and I was in luck. I bumped into someone else from the show and he knew which office Archie worked in. I'd never gone into one of the offices like his and was a bit hesitant. He smiled when he saw me and quickly guided me back out into the corridor. I assumed that was in case I saw or heard something I shouldn't. I felt disloyal telling him the problem I faced with Grant, but he'd seen enough to understand my dilemma. Within five minutes, he assured me he'd find a way to get Grant to the show. The worst that could happen wasn't bad at all – the veterans would have a good time. We'd sweet-talked the canteen ladies into making some sandwich and cakes, so it would be a real treat for them.

The rest of the day dragged as often happened when you're itching to get somewhere else. I was relieved no more transmissions were suddenly cut off and hoped all the courageous people using the radios were safe.

* * *

It was dark again by the time I reached Grant's place – a ground-floor flat which was half a terraced house. I had to use my shielded torch to make sure I was in the right place. The door had once been dark blue, but was scratched down to the bare wood round the keyhole. I spent a moment trying to pluck up the courage to knock and was surprised to hear voices inside. Was Archie with him? Would I be spoiling the conversation about the veterans' show? I dithered, wondering what to do, then told myself off for being such a coward.

I knocked and stepped back, barely able to breathe.

Footsteps echoed inside – no sound of crutches thumping on the lino – and I wondered who would answer the door. To my surprise, it was a woman. An older woman, very elegant. She wore a battleship-grey dress with a short red jacket over the top. Her greying hair was set in immaculate curls. Once upon a time, I would have been nervous of someone like her, someone from a high class. But a lot of time had passed since I lived with my parents in grotty rooms in Coventry. More importantly, life had given me a massive variety of experiences and people to deal with.

But her welcoming smile was what made it easier to feel comfortable with her. 'Can I help you?'

I swallowed and smiled back. 'I've come to see Grant. I'm his girlfriend, Lily.' As I said it I wondered if I was still his girlfriend, or if he'd given me the push without actually saying so.

Her smile widened. 'So you're Lily! I'm so glad to meet you. Grant has mentioned you. I'm his mother, Mrs Frankland. Do come in.'

I stepped inside the hall and noticed that the door to the living room was closed. Mrs Frankland put her fingers to her lips and whispered, 'I'm glad you're here. He needs cheering up. See what you can do.'

She led the way, and I followed her in. Grant was sitting on a small sofa, his crutches propped up against one arm. He was reading a newspaper. I saw the headline said, 'US Bombs Italy'. He looked up when we came in and gave a half-smile. No one would say it was an enthusiastic welcome.

'Grant, Lily's come to see you. I'll leave you two together and make some tea.'

I thought she'd probably be a long time doing it to leave us to talk. I looked around the room. The decor was dated, flowery wallpaper, which couldn't have been Grant's choice. The furniture was serviceable but faded. But like me, he probably had no hand in choosing his billet.

I went to sit next to him and put my hand on his arm. Pain had etched lines on his face that weren't there before his accident. 'Hello, darling. I've missed you,' I said.

I hoped he would respond, but apart from folding up his newspaper, he did nothing. While I was full of sympathy for what had happened to him, so dreadful, I found myself getting irritated, my face tightening and my shoulders tensing. He was an intelligent man, I thought. Surely he could snap himself out of it. But immediately I felt enormous guilt at those thoughts. If it was easy to snap out of his mood, his depression, he'd have done it. He wasn't being like this for pleasure. I remembered everything I'd been told about people who'd experience something traumatic. His reaction was normal in the circumstances.

'Talk to me, Grant,' I said. 'Your mum said I'm your girlfriend, but at the moment, I don't even know if that's true.'

'I'll be back at work tomorrow,' he said without looking at me. It wasn't the answer I wanted, but at least he was speaking.

'That's wonderful. I'm sure your unit has missed you. I know I have.' I wanted to ask if he was really ready, but suspected that question would irritate him. Instead of seeing it as a loving question from someone who cared for him, he might see it as interfering, nagging even. I decided that instead of trying to open up, I'd simply chat about the panto, Peggy's niece and other bits and pieces of news.

His mother returned with a tray of tea and biscuits. 'It sounds as if you have a busy life,' she said.

We talked for another twenty minutes or so and then I made an excuse and stood to leave. Grant didn't try to stop me, but I bent over and kissed him on the cheek. 'Goodbye, my love,' I whispered in his ear.

Rain had begun while I was with him. It came down so hard it almost hurt, stinging any skin exposed. In the distance, I saw a flash of lightning and automatically counted the seconds. Seven. The eye of the storm was still a little way away, or perhaps avoiding Bletchley altogether. I trudged towards home wishing I'd thought to bring an umbrella, not that it would have done much good in the fierce wind. Head down, I was soon totally soaked and shivering.

Gloomy thoughts followed me all the way, and I looked forward to the oblivion of sleep.

10

'LOOK BEHIND YOU!'

Those of us with no acting part at that moment of the panto rehearsal were enjoying watching the actors on stage. We couldn't resist joining in as children did with 'OH YES, YOU DID!' and 'OH NO, YOU DIDN'T!' as well as 'LOOK BEHIND YOU!'

It wasn't the dress rehearsal yet, but some of the cast were already wearing all or part of their costume. Inevitably, there was a delay starting the rehearsal. Some people were late – always the same people – and they got short shrift when they delayed things for the third time. As the rehearsal went on, I was glad I wasn't Archie, the director. George, as the pantomime dame, couldn't resist ad-libbing. No one would have minded that if his comments were funny, but unfortunately they weren't. Archie would have to have a quiet word with him.

Carolyn was watching from the wings and I saw her wince a few times. Then there were the people who forgot their lines, sometimes people with very few lines to say. Then Jane, who was playing Mary Quite Contrary, lived up to her name. She seemed to be making a power play to take over directing the whole thing. *I think it would be better if we stood here! Surely Mother Goose should speak in a different voice! You need to give clearer instructions!* Each time she picked holes in something, the whole panto ground to a halt, and the flow was broken. Archie's nostrils flared and his teeth were bared in an effort to respond politely.

Bronwyn saved the day. 'Not joking, or nothing, Jane,' she said loudly enough for everyone to hear, 'but why don't you just get on with your job and let Archie get on with his? You're holding everybody up!'

Jane's eyes widened as she absorbed what Bronwyn had said, then she threw down the shepherdess's crook she was holding and stomped off. 'I won't be back!' she shouted as she slammed the door hard enough to make it rattle. I heard a few people mutter, 'Thank goodness!'

The atmosphere in the room, which had been tense since the start, relaxed, and everyone looked more comfortable.

But I was Jane's understudy. Would Archie ask me to step in? He did.

'Right, I can't be doing with that,' he said, struggling to calm his breathing. 'Jane's out of the cast. Pity. Lily, do you know her lines? We can manage without your bit part.'

Luckily, I did know the lines, although I'd never expected to use them. Lines were only part of what was needed, though. I had to practise timing, gestures, facial expressions and where to stand at any one time.

It was only when I got up on stage that I noticed Grant at the back of the room. He was sitting down, his crutches beside him. He certainly didn't look like he was enjoying himself much, but at least he was there, and I took that as a positive step forward. I longed to run over to him, but couldn't desert the stage. When I next looked, he was gone.

When I was off stage, I stood by Carolyn and we had whispered conversations. 'What do you think of George as Mother Goose?' I asked.

She smiled. 'I'm amazed. It's a whole other side of him, he's usually so sensible and proper.'

'Is that okay with you?'

She nodded. 'It is. Definitely. Tickety-boo. If we stay together, and that's by no means certain, it means we can have more fun. I worried our relationship would be too serious all the time.'

Eventually, the rehearsal ground to a halt. It was so far off perfect it was frightening, but even with my limited theatrical experience I was beginning to understand that wasn't unusual.

'Right, gang,' Archie shouted after clapping his hands to get attention. 'Who's coming over to the Beer Hut? I'm buying the first round!'

I was delighted to see Thomas in the Beer Hut. Bronwyn was still keeping very quiet about whether her relationship with him was going anywhere. But he smiled when he spotted her, walked over, and offered us both a drink.

Peggy was busy serving. It was the first night all four of us were off duty at the same time and Mrs W. had kindly offered to look after Linda. She'd gradually built a relationship with her, mostly around biscuits.

'I 'ad a letter from Marion today,' Peggy said between pouring pints. 'She's no better, still gotta rest all the time.'

'But no worse?' I asked.

'If she is, she ain't said. The doctor says the baby is growing okay, so that's a blessing.' She looked around. 'No Grant then?'

My shoulders sagged. 'He came to the rehearsal for a few minutes, then vanished. I don't know if he's back at work or at home.'

She was interrupted by a tall, grumpy-looking man ordering

four pints of bitter. He'd been waving a ten-bob note around as if that entitled him to anything he wanted. 'If this bloke drinks much more every day 'e won't live long, I can tell you,' Peggy said when she'd served him. Of course, he didn't thank her. 'Pity Grant's not 'ere. Bronwyn's with 'er bloke and Carolyn's with George. You and me are the old maids.'

I grinned. 'I don't feel like an old maid and you certainly don't look like one!'

* * *

It had been a good night at the Duck and Goose, and I'd unwisely had a bit too much to drink. Several of the panto folk were there, and so there was plenty of clowning around. The place was packed, and I was squashed between two other girls. Conversation was hampered by general noise: darts being thrown, card players shouting triumphantly; glasses clattering and the outside door opening and closing. By halfway through the evening, I was having to shout to be heard, and that, coupled with the cigarette smoke, made my throat sore. I finished my shandy and stood up.

'I'm off, early start tomorrow. Thanks for the drink, Archie!'

I put on my coat, scarf, mittens and bobble hat and went outside. Even though Bletchley was spared bombing, it still had the same blackout regulations as London. That meant walking at night was treacherous. I used my torch, and was helped by the shielded car lights to find my way, but still made slow progress. After a short time, my eyes adjusted to the dark, and I decided to take a little detour to clear my head before going home.

As I walked, I became aware that things looked different in the gloom, and the cold air felt damp and clammy. It took me a couple of minutes to realise it was fog creeping up from the direction of the river, joining smoke from the many chimneys. The fog surrounded me and the buildings stealthily, like a cat stalking its prey, silent, slow, cunning. It wrapped itself round lampposts, sneaked under benches, flowed over gates. The sounds of cars, of a horse and cart, of footsteps, became muffled, and before long I had to struggle to be sure where I was. As fog does, it swirled, one minute making it hard to see a yard in front of my face, another able to see further away.

Fortunately, Bletchley Town had its fair share of pubs. Blackout curtains on doors should have hidden the light when they were opened. But chinks of light escaped as if they couldn't stand being indoors. They helped guide me on my way. As I walked, I went over my panto lines in my head, remembering those and all the other things I had to do to give a good performance.

I was walking along a street that edged the park and there was a public toilet close by. Footsteps from that direction got my attention. Not expecting to see anything because of the fog, I still turned my head that way. For a second the fog cleared and what I saw made me gasp.

George, Carolyn's boyfriend, was coming out of the toilet with another man.

They were holding hands.

I was so stunned I didn't notice a dog running across my path and fell over it, landing on my knees and hands. 'Damn!' I swore, sitting in the damp rubbing my knee and ruined stockings. But before I could stand up, I was pulled upright by two strong sets of hands.

'Oh Lily, it's you!' George said. The fog had eddied back again and I could barely make out his face, but his voice demonstrated worry.

I pulled my clothes straight and thanked him. There was an awkward pause as we looked at each other.

'Lily, this is my friend... Henry. Henry, this is Lily. She's a friend of Carolyn's.' He looked everywhere but at me.

He held out his hand. 'Pleased to meet you,' he said, sounding very strained.

Another awkward silence, then George said, 'Did you see...' he asked. Although he gestured towards the toilets, he never said what he was referring to. He didn't need to.

'Isn't the fog awful?' I said. 'No wonder I tripped over that wretched dog. I couldn't see a thing.'

It may have been my imagination, but I thought I heard him sigh with relief. 'Do you want me to walk you home?' he said. 'You must be a bit shaken.'

His friend was still there, and I couldn't imagine having to make small talk in the circumstances. 'No, I'm fine. I'll look like a schoolkid tomorrow with a grazed knee, that's all. Thank you both for your help.'

After a couple of minutes reassuring themselves I was okay, they left, definitely not holding hands.

I began walking again, cursing that the 'starlight' lights that the council promised to replace street lights had never materialised. But I was relieved when I almost bumped into an air raid protection volunteer.

'You okay, love?' she asked. 'Only I thought I heard someone cry out, but couldn't work out where the sound was coming from.'

'It was me, I fell over a dog. Couldn't see it in this rotten fog.'

'Tell me, a whole German troop could come down the High Street in this and we wouldn't be able to see them.'

'We'd hear them though!' I said with a laugh.

'Trust me, some of the older ARP wardens are so deaf, even that's doubtful. It's nice to have someone to talk to. Where are you going?'

'Home. It's only a couple of streets away.'

'Mind if I walk with you? Not much for me to do apart from shouting at people who've got lights showing. Not like we ever get bombed. It's dead boring here. I thought if I became a warden there would be all sorts of excitement. Rescuing people from burning buildings and that sort of thing. Not being called a little Hitler when I remind them about the regulations.'

I was still feeling a bit shaky after my fall, so I was glad of her company. 'Trust me, I've had to rescue more people than I want to remember. You're better off being bored. Do many people have lights showing? I don't see many.'

She laughed. 'Well, the worst was last winter when it was snowing. Would you believe one bloke had a greenhouse in his back garden? He only left a light on all night to melt the snow so his plants wouldn't get too cold. What a fat head! He was very indignant when I told him to turn it off. I thought he was going to thump me!'

The walk was slower than usual because of the fog, and by the time she left me at home it was as if we'd known each other for ages. Despite that, I was glad to be alone to think about what I'd seen. Had George really been holding the other man's hand? Had they needed to go to the toilet at the same time, or had something else been happening? Was his friend's name really Henry? He was a lot older than George and had an accent I couldn't place.

If George was seeing another man, he was taking so much risk. If he was found out, he'd be prosecuted and probably imprisoned. As I made a cup of cocoa to take to bed, I pondered again on whether to tell Carolyn. Some people say that if you tell someone something bad about their loved one, they'll either not believe you or hate you. Or possibly both.

My dreams that night were full of monsters. It was as if I were a child again, seeing monsters under the bed and inside the wardrobe. I tossed and turned and must have woken up three times in all.

I hoped that by the next day I'd think the whole incident had been a nightmare.

11

Peggy and I rarely had the same day off, but for once it happened. I'd been responsible for little Linda a few times, picking her up from nursery school, giving her her tea and putting her to bed. She was a cheerful girl once she'd got used to us, and mostly a pleasure to be with. She had the occasional tantrum, demanding to be taken to her mother and repeating that Peggy wasn't her mum. But tantrums at that age are common. Or so Mrs W. assured me. She had taken to the child and liked to pop in from time to time. Of course, she had a biscuit every time and sometimes found a small toy for Linda to play with. She had a ball, and a set of jacks that she wasn't really old enough to use properly yet. She enjoyed trying, though. A neighbour had given her a doll and Bronwyn was busy knitting doll's clothes. We had cards to play Snap as well as some books I'd got at the jumble sale.

We all headed to the park when she got restless indoors, and played ball – we certainly needed something active to keep us warm on the cold December day. There was a clear blue sky, but the wind forced its way through our clothes. Boys were playing football, and some mums were pushing their babies in their massive Silver Cross prams. The bandstand looked forlorn and neglected, hardly recognisable from the summer days when a brass band played and bystanders enjoyed their music.

After playing ball, we went to the play area. Some of the things that were made of metal had been taken away for the war effort. But a few still remained – a solitary swing, a roundabout and a slide.

Linda tugged at Peggy's hand. 'Roundabout! Roundabout!' I remembered loving them myself when I was a child. The slight dizziness felt a bit dangerous, but we all laughed at the sensation, anyway.

A little boy, maybe three years older than Linda, joined her on the roundabout. 'Bet I can push it on my own!' he said. 'I'm tough!' We'd been pushing it for Linda. She was too small to do it herself. At first, his enthusiasm seemed harmless, just a way of showing off. But then he got faster and faster and Linda's face crumpled, her bottom lip trembling, ready for tears. She'd been holding onto the bars with her mittened hands and I noticed they were slipping with the movement.

'Slow down!' I shouted at the lad two or three times, but he wasn't taking any notice. Peggy and I looked at each other, our thoughts in harmony. We stepped forward and made a grab for the arms of the roundabout to slow it down.

What we didn't know was Linda had stopped holding on.

She flew off as if a giant hand had pushed her, and landed on one elbow. There was a terrible cracking noise. Her screams were probably heard all over Bletchley.

Aghast, we ran over to her. She was lying on the floor, one arm dangling as if it no longer belonged to her body.

'Ohmyword!' Peggy said, terror in her eyes. 'I reckon she's gone and broke it. What'll we do?'

'Hospital,' I replied. 'We need to get her to a hospital. I'll carry her.' I helped her to sit up, and using my scarf, rested her arm against her side. She howled the whole time, but I saw we needed to stop it moving more. I'd had first aid training when I was with the ARP.

As I walked to the road, I glanced at the boy who had been the cause of the trouble. He was still spinning round as if nothing had happened, oblivious to the harm he had done.

We waited a couple of minutes by the roadside, then got lucky and a taxi came along.

'Shouldn't we wait for an ambulance?' Peggy said. 'Taxis are so dear.'

'It's not far and we need to get her help quickly. I'll pay.'

She nodded and kissed Linda on the cheek again and again. 'You'll be tickety-boo in no time,' she said. 'I bet them doctors'll put a big plaster on your arm and all your friends'll be dead jealous.'

The taxi dropped us off at the door of the emergency department, and I was grateful we wouldn't have to make her walk far. Or carry her. We found a wheelchair just inside the department and gently put Linda in it. She'd stopped screaming, but her face was worryingly white and she was gritting her teeth. I thought she might faint.

The nurse who saw her was kindness itself, with her rosy-red cheeks and a lovely smile. She took one look at Linda's arm and said, 'Oh my goodness, you've really hurt yourself, haven't you!' She took hold of the wheelchair and wheeled her off to X-ray, with us following. 'When the results come through, a doctor will see you,' she said. She'd given Linda a boiled sweet, and that stopped her crying for a while. I wished I'd thought of that.

It was an agonising wait for the diagnosis. While we waited, I looked around at the notices on the wall. One showed an ARP warden blowing a whistle and said, 'In a raid – open your door to passers-by – they need shelter too.' Another showed a carrot with a smiling face. 'A carrot a day keeps the doctor away', it read. A third showed a man sneezing into an enormous handkerchief. 'Coughs and sneezes spread diseases. A handkerchief in time saves nine.' The nine were members of the various forces.

'Yes, definitely a broken radius bone,' the doctor said when he returned. 'Which of you is her mother?'

'They're not my mum!' Linda cried. 'I want my mum!'

Peggy had gone almost as white as Linda, and held back as I'd seen her do before.

I had to step in. 'This is Linda's aunt. She's looking after Linda while her mum is unwell,' I said.

He turned to Peggy. 'We really like to have a parent's permission when we treat children. Is her mother nearby? Could she sign the relevant form?'

Peggy shook her head. She looked a bit dazed. 'She lives a long way away, and she's not well.'

'I see. Then we'll have to do the best we can. I presume you give permission for us to treat your niece? We'll give her some painkillers and put a plaster on her arm.'

Peggy seemed to snap out of whatever was going on with her. 'Of course I do,' she said, and held Linda's good hand. While the doctor was putting on the plaster, we tried to distract the little girl with chat. She noticed a Christmas decoration on the wall.

'Aunty Peg, will we go to see my mum for Christmas?'

Peggy hesitated. 'I can't promise, my love. But if it is possible, we will.'

I knew she'd have to make sure Marion was well enough for visitors and also get two days off work. Neither of those was a given.

That night in bed, I realised I thought myself an honest person. Yet I'd lied over and over again about little Linda's parentage. My conscience struggled with this thought. But eventually I decided that sometimes telling a lie does less harm than telling the truth. It was strange seeing Peggy act as she had been with Linda, one minute warm and the next remote. She was usually so bouncy and cheerful.

What would this time spent with Linda do to her when she had to give her back?

12

I knew Grant was back at work and had seen him briefly at the rehearsal, but we still hadn't had a chance to talk. I didn't feel it would be right going to his home again, so work was my best chance of seeing him. The trouble was, I had no way of finding out when his breaks were. And in any case, he might not go to the canteen or the Beer Hut because of the struggle on his crutches.

I put on my coat and headed towards the canteen. As I went, I saw someone riding a bike out of the park wearing a full gas mask. I gaped at the sight. We all carried gas masks in boxes, but we certainly didn't wear them. The man was well known in the Park, and I'd been told his name was Alan Turing, reputed to be an eccentric genius. It sometimes felt as if the place was full of them.

We'd had a memo telling us to be more careful with the crockery. It baffled me at first until I spotted cups and saucers in odd places, like under or even in bushes and trees. Once, I even saw a cup and saucer gliding across the lake like some strange boat. And it wasn't unusual to see the clever bods standing by the lake, deep in thought. Then some of them would throw their cup into the lake and shout 'Yes!' Mrs W. would have a fit if she lost crockery at half the rate it disappeared at the Park.

Picking up a cup that had been left on the front step of the big house, I walked towards the canteen. I was delighted, but scared, when I bumped into Grant heading the same way. He was moving slowly and painfully on his crutches, and I wondered how much he used the wheelchair, which was outside what I presumed was his office. Surely, it would give him a break from pain. But his stubbornness showed what a brave man he was, and how determined to get his life back to normal.

Apart from our relationship.

I had butterflies in my stomach as I caught up with him and said hello. He was at a disadvantage. He could hardly run away. 'Come on,' I said, 'let's have our break together.'

He gave a strained smile, but didn't speak. At least he didn't tell me to go away. Not a word passed between us as we queued for our food. I chose potato and bacon hotpot and Grant asked for beef stew with dumplings. He hopped along the counter with both crutches in one hand, pushing his tray as he went. I hesitated to offer to help in case he thought I was trying to undermine him. But I took the tray off him when he needed to go to a table. He indicated where he wanted to sit and I put his tray down, then went back for my own.

Having a private conversation in the canteen was difficult. The sounds of crockery, cutlery and so many voices made it impossible to speak quietly. I decided the best bet was to talk about anything other than us.

'How is your leg healing?' I asked.

He finished chewing his mouthful of tough beef. 'The doctors say it's doing really well. Faster than usual.' It was something.

Before I could respond, someone on the other side of him

began asking him a question. I half listened, but mostly my mind was on what was going wrong. Had Grant gone off me? Had I done something wrong or something that made him think differently about me? Questions like these went round and round in my mind, as they had many times since he'd been injured. I got no nearer to an answer though, and could feel my confidence in myself and our future seeping away. But I'd spoken to Bronwyn about it several times, and she assured me that it couldn't be anything I'd done. After all, Grant's distant behaviour began when he was in hospital.

I shook myself out of these negative thoughts and listened to his conversation with the other man. I noticed his answers were briefer than they used to be and he didn't seem fully engaged, just going through the motions.

Suddenly I felt angry.

Enough was enough.

I left the table and went back into the corridor. There I grabbed Grant's wheelchair and pushed it towards the canteen, glad to see there was a blanket on it.

He looked up in surprise when I stopped by his seat. I picked up his crutches and put them in the chair. 'Come on, Grant, we're going to get some fresh air,' I said in a quiet voice, but one that showed I meant business. He looked at me, then at the wheelchair, a confused frown on his brow.

Bending over, I helped him up. Looking dazed, he manoeuvred himself into the chair and I put the rug over his knees. 'It's sunny outside, so I thought we could go for a walk round the lake.'

There was no way of knowing if he was too baffled to argue, or too angry. Either way, he said nothing until we were outside and away from people.

I soon realised that one advantage of pushing someone in a

wheelchair and talking to them is you don't have to talk face to face. Sometimes face to face is good, but it can also be a hindrance. People can feel exposed if you can see them. Grant sat unmoving, his hands folded on the rug.

'Right, Grant,' I said, keeping my voice low and warm. 'You've been avoiding me, and when you see me, you've been distant.' As I spoke, my stomach felt hollow, and for a minute it was as if everything around us had vanished. I heard the blood pounding in my ears and had to ask him to repeat his answer.

'I said I'm not a whole man. You wouldn't want part of a man.'

His answer made me furious, and I stuttered as I replied. 'You stupid man. I bet you'd feel the same about me if I lost half a leg, wouldn't you! You wouldn't think I was only part of a woman.'

There was a pause, then he slowly nodded.

'Then why wouldn't I feel the same about you? I didn't only love that bit of your leg, you idiot.'

Immediately, I felt I shouldn't have been so harsh, but I'd been very patient and I was allowed to have feelings too.

'You don't understand...' he began.

'If I don't understand, it's because you haven't explained how you feel.'

As I spoke, one of the boffins who'd been stock-still on the other side of the lake shouted, 'Got it!' and threw his cup in the water.

'See how easily that cup was thrown away? That's how your behaviour has left me feeling. As if I'm worthless and not worth keeping. You've suffered something terrible, that's for sure, but it's time to let yourself feel hope for the future again.'

As we spoke, I'd been slowly pushing him round the lake – not easy on the gravel. Geese picked at the cold grass on its edge and birds sat in the trees hoping to spot something tasty to eat. All the lilies that were so abundant in the summer had long gone, and the lake looked forlorn, deserted. The sharp wind had dropped, but the air was still cold and I became aware that my midday break was coming to an end. I'd be in trouble if I didn't get back soon.

Grant still hadn't spoken, but I noticed the tension in his shoulders had relaxed. 'I'm going to push you back to your office now, Grant, or I'll be late back. Let me know what you want to do. You can either end our relationship or we move forward. I can't take any more of this.'

In response, he didn't say anything, but he leaned back and put his hand over one of mine.

* * *

It was eight o'clock in the morning and Bronwyn and I had been on duty since midnight. The radios were quieter than usual, probably because most of France was in the same time zone as us, despite Hitler making the country change to German time. But they weren't quiet enough to catch a nap, apart from five or ten minutes in our breaks.

We handed over our equipment to the next shift and pulled on our hats, coats, and scarves. Stepping outside into the winter morning, I took a deep breath of fresh air. The sun was waking up from its deep well of winter, but it was still cold enough to make me shiver.

'Come on,' Bronwyn said, heading towards the big house. 'Do you remember we're going to get my fairy costume so you can make it fit properly?'

The only thing I truly wanted to do was get the next bus and fall into my bed, warm and snug under the blankets. But going to the props room and getting the dress off the hanger wouldn't take long so I could hardly object.

The corridors in the big house were coming to life with the change of shift. We heard creaks from the floor above, a chair scraping back, doors opening and closing, and the pipes warming up.

Half asleep, we pushed a door to the props room and turned on the light. The bright colours of the costumes were in sharp contrast to the dimly lit corridors, making us blink.

'Right,' Bronwyn said, getting a bag from her rucksack. 'Let's get this dress and run for the bus.' But it wasn't to be.

The dress wasn't there.

The props room was orderly. It had to be because, as well as a massive variety of costumes, it had other props from jewellery to furniture, paintings to vases, shoes to hats. So we knew where the dress should have been. It wasn't there.

'What?' Bronwyn said and began frantically pushing aside other dresses. 'Some idiot must have put it in the wrong place.'

We spent ages going through everything. Under other outfits, in boxes of hats, gloves, swords and all sorts of things I couldn't imagine ever being used. No one had put it in the wrong place.

It wasn't there.

Someone had taken it.

* * *

We'd missed our planned bus and had to stand in the cold morning waiting for the next one, dejected and puzzled. 'Could someone have taken it away to be cleaned or repaired?' I wondered.

Bronwyn shook her head. 'They always leave a note where the item should be. They're really good about that.'

We were both too dog-tired to talk about it more and the swaying of the bus soon lulled me to sleep. The conductor had asked us where we wanted to get off when we boarded. She was used to seeing people at the Park looking half asleep at that time of the morning. We were both so sleepy she had to shake us awake at our stop. 'Come on, sleepyheads!' she said with a smile.

Rubbing my eyes, I followed Bronwyn off the bus.

'It's Jane!' she said as soon as we stepped onto the pavement. 'My brain worked it out while I was asleep.'

We began walking towards Happy Days. 'What do you mean, it's Jane? What are you talking about?'

'My fairy dress. I'd bet a penny to a pound she took the dress.'

I was getting my key out of my bag. 'You've lost me. Who's Jane?'

'Remember that woman who was pushing her weight around at one of the first rehearsals? I told her to leave Archie to do his job, and she stormed off. I bet it's her. She looked at me as if she wanted me dead, and every time I see her around the Park, she glares at me.' By now, we were inside and glad to be out of the cold. Glad too, that we couldn't hear Mrs W. pottering about in the kitchen. It wasn't that we minded her, but she could be hard to get rid of and we just wanted toast and sleep.

Hanging up our coats, I asked, 'What shall we do? Tackle her?'

'Not being funny or nothing, but why wouldn't we? If she didn't take it, we'll be able to tell. If she did, we'll make her give it back. I'm going to need that dress in a couple of days. I can hardly go on stage wearing only the wings.'

The fire had gone out in the kitchen, so we wasted no time with our tea and toast. 'Do you know what shifts she's on at the moment?' I asked.

Bronwyn sipped her tea. 'I'm pretty sure she's on early shift. If we go in good time, we should catch her. That's if you don't mind coming with me.'

'Are you kidding? I wouldn't miss it for the world.'

* * *

Our shift was due to start at four o'clock, so we got there in good time. Bronwyn knew which hut Jane worked in, so we headed towards it. Jane would be leaving at four, so we waited outside her hut from ten to. We could hear choral singing from the big house, no doubt a group getting ready for a concert somewhere. A man walked by holding a chess set and another walked towards the Beer Hut, looking exhausted and in need of a drink.

As the time crept towards four o'clock, I could feel myself getting tense. I hated confrontation, but knew we had to sort this out or poor Bronwyn would be stuck for the panto. All her hard work for nothing. And what would we do? Her part was important, she'd have to have something to wear. Something suitable.

At last Jane appeared. She seemed not to notice us at first and made to walk straight past. Bronwyn didn't hesitate. She stepped in front of her.

'My fairy dress for the panto is missing. Would you happen to know anything about that, Jane?' Her back was straight and her eyes blazing.

Jane took a step back. 'What? What are you talking about? What dress?' She may have thought she looked innocent, but her face gave her away.

Bronwyn glared at her. 'My fairy dress. I need it. Is this your idea of revenge because I told you to lay off Archie at the rehearsal?'

Jane tried to walk past us, but we moved to block her again. Stamping her foot, she put her hands on her hips. 'Oh, that. I'd forgotten all about it. I didn't want to be in the stupid panto, anyway. It's going to be a big flop. Everyone says it was stupid giving you that part. You've no acting experience, and I've never seen anyone look less like a fairy.'

Bronwyn drew in her breath. 'And I've never seen anyone look as guilty as you do now. So where's my dress, you vindictive cow?'

Jane drew back her fist, ready to strike out, but just then one of her colleagues walked past. 'Everything okay, Jane?' she asked.

'Fine!' Her tone said the other woman should go away. With a shrug, she did.

'Right, so give me the dress or I'll report you to the Commander right now,' Bronwyn said, her voice dripping ice.

As if a tap had been turned off, Jane crumbled. Being reported to the Commander was not a threat to be ignored lightly.

'I've burned it,' she whispered.

Bronwyn's eyes opened wide with disbelief. 'WHAT DID YOU SAY? YOU'VE BURNED IT? ARE YOU OUT OF YOUR FRIGGING MIND?' Bronwyn bellowed. Her voice echoed around the lake, and some ducks flew off in terror.

Jane nodded, her head down and shoulders slumped. 'Yes, I did.' Then she looked up, defiant. 'So you won't have it, will you! You won't look pretty and get everyone's attention, will you!'

I stared at her, open-mouthed. So it wasn't just about revenge for Bronwyn's words. It was jealousy because of her good looks. What a sad girl she was. I almost felt sorry for her. Almost.

She attempted to walk past us again, and we let her go.

'I'm tamping!' Bronwyn said. 'I've a good mind to report her right now.'

I held her arm. 'It's time for us to start our shift. Let's talk about it during the break. Don't do anything too rash.'

It was halfway through our shifts before we both had a break at the same time.

'Beer Hut or canteen?' I asked as we wrapped up warm.

Bronwyn sighed. 'Canteen.'

The ducks were back, quacking and looking for food as usual. 'Glad your shouting didn't make them leave the country!' I joked, and she poked her tongue out at me like a five-year-old.

The frosty gravel crunched under our feet and we heard a car horn in the distance blaring. 'Someone's in a bad mood,' Bronwyn said.

We'd reached the queue for tea. 'What about you?' I asked. 'Are you still in a bad mood?'

She picked up a cup and scowled at the brown liquid. 'I'm not going to report her, if that's what you mean. She deserves it, mind. But that doesn't help me find a dress.'

I led her to a couple of seats. 'I had an idea for that.'

Her face brightened. 'You have? Not joking or nothing?'

I nodded. 'Do you remember when Carolyn invited us to her party at the Savoy ages ago? Mrs W. loaned us a couple of evening dresses.'

She nodded, following my drift. 'And you made them fit us perfectly.'

Another motorcycle messenger roared past, screeching to a halt outside the window where we stood. He must have scattered gravel everywhere.

'Well, why don't we ask her if we can borrow one again? They're beautiful and with some bits of ribbon and stuff to make them look less serious. I think they'll do the trick.'

She put her cup down and threw her arms around me. 'Lil, you're a flipping genius! Let's ask her in the morning.'

Mrs W. came up trumps and loaned Bronwyn the blue dress she'd worn before, with many warnings to take care of it. It still fitted perfectly. Later the next day I enjoyed rummaging through all my odd bits of ribbon, lace and buttons. Mum had given me a half of hers ages ago, and sometimes if a cardigan or blouse was going for pennies at a jumble sale because it was well past it, I'd buy it just for the trimmings. Linda helped me make bows and rosettes as best she could with one arm in plaster, and demanded a ribbon for her hair. She was too young to do much, but I gave her the smallest scraps and she enjoyed fiddling with them, exclaiming how pretty the colours were. Placing all the trimmings needed care so that the stitches wouldn't show once they were taken off.

When I'd finished, Bronwyn tried it on, and twirled round in front of the mirror, pretending to have a wand. 'Mirror, mirror, on the wall, who's the fairest of them all?'

I laughed. 'Well, Jane thinks you are! And she's right!'

13

Carolyn had done a wonderful job organising the show for the town's veterans. They were mostly from the Boar and Great Wars, although there were a few from less well-known conflicts. Some were regular soldiers who had had illnesses or accidents that meant they were medically discharged.

The Veterans' Club in Bletchley Town was the obvious venue for the show. London was big enough to have several clubs, each dedicated to a specific group. Bletchley wasn't that big, but its Veterans' Club was active. They loved having shows or similar, sometimes singers, sometimes magicians, sometimes talks. The main hall would be just about big enough for the expected numbers. They would provide refreshments.

We were performing the panto for the men, even though it was far from perfect. We hoped they'd be kind to us as it was free and they'd get refreshments. Already in my costume, I peered through a window as the men arrived. I was shocked at the variation in ages of the veterans. I'd expected them to be very old, white hair, walking sticks, bent as they walked. But I had to quickly do the maths. Men in the Great War who signed up while young could be in their forties or even younger. That would be especially true if they'd lied about their age to get in as many did. But veterans of the Boer War would be much older.

I sneaked through to another room where I could see them being admitted. Almost every man was wearing war medals and quite a few wore their uniform caps, too. If they'd be able to enter more quickly, I'm sure they'd have marched.

The hall was ready with rows of chairs and a place at each end for wheelchairs. The maroon velvet curtains were pulled closed in readiness for the opening.

Then I spotted the desk where they gave their name and my jaw dropped open. The person taking their names was none other than Grant. He was sitting on a normal chair, his crutches beside him and a wheelchair nearby. I smiled. Archie had been as good as his word and got Grant there in a role where he could feel useful.

But then I overheard the conversations of the men as they came in and my high hopes crashed. At least a quarter of them asked Grant where he'd got his injury, despite him wearing no medals. All assumed it was a war injury, obtained in action. He had to explain again and again that he'd been caught in an air raid. The common response was 'Oh!' as if that ended the conversation, although they still smiled and several of them shook his hand or even saluted to him.

It was true that a fair number of the audience were obviously injured. Four were in wheelchairs, three on crutches, four with one arm missing, and two blind men were guided by others. Some of the older men clearly had trouble hearing.

But the one thing they all had in common was cheerfulness. It was an outing for them, and they would meet old comrades and spend an afternoon enjoyably. And they'd get fed.

Leaving it to the last minute to return backstage, I watched

Grant's reaction to his task. At first, the look on his face showed he was shocked, but gradually that changed. As more and more men chatted to him, sometimes causing a backlog, he relaxed and smiled. It was the best smile I'd seen from him for ages and it made my heart sing.

I didn't let him see me, but headed backstage, ready for the show to start. I could hear the audience chatting and was relieved that the atmosphere seemed lively and positive.

Archie introduced the show.

'Gentlemen, we are delighted to offer you this year's panto, *Mother Goose*. You'll enjoy it!'

He grinned at the audience and lifted up his arms, urging them to respond.

'OH NO, WE WON'T!' came the reply.

'First an apology – this is also a dress rehearsal, so forgive us if it's not up to scratch. The show will be in two halves with a refreshment break in the middle. And before the second half, we have a special treat. Peggy Kent – who is the most important person at Bletchley Park; she's the barmaid! – will be inviting you to sing along with her with some old familiar numbers.'

Considering how few rehearsals we had had the first half went well. The 'horse' fell over twice and looked idiotic trying to get up. The audience thought it was deliberate and loved it. Luckily, the two men in the horse's outfit didn't fall off the stage this time. George, as Mother Goose, hammed it up for all he was worth and got a lot of laughs, especially when he hitched up his bosom and talked to the audience as if he was talking to a neighbour over a fence. At one point when his character was in trouble, he started singing 'Pack Up Your Troubles in Your Old Kit Bag' and within seconds the whole audience was singing along with him.

I was relieved to remember all my lines, or well enough that the joins didn't show. As had happened before, stage fright made me tremble before I went on, but once I'd said the first couple of lines, a sort of euphoria took over and I thoroughly enjoyed it.

All too soon the first half was over. We'd decided to have a longish interval. It gave us time to give the veterans tea and biscuits and talk to them. Bronwyn, myself and a couple of other members of the cast went out to chat with them. Bronwyn soon had to take off her wings, or she was in danger of doing someone an injury.

I sat next to an elderly man who was sitting on his own. He had a stick beside him and only one arm. He displayed a chest full of medals.

'Are you enjoying it?' I asked.

'I am, ducks. It's a right good laugh. You folks here at the Park always put on a good show.'

Someone handed him a cup and saucer and I realised that he couldn't possibly drink the tea like that. He needed a mug, and ideally somewhere to put it. 'Here,' I said, 'let me take the saucer.'

'Thanks, Ducks. People think I lost this arm in the Boer War, being brave and heroic. Truth is, five years after I came out of the army, I was doing some work on my house. I fell from a ladder, right from the top. Amazing I've still got a brain! In hospital for ages, I was.'

'Gosh, that must have been awful. It must have taken you a long time to adjust.'

'Not kidding. But my missus was wonderful and we get by.' Another veteran came over to speak to him and I moved on, trying to have a word with as many of them as possible. I'd found most men didn't want to speak about their experiences, especially during the Great War. Many of them had never recovered mentally, and we heard stories of special hospitals where they lived, unable to return to normal life. But the men at the panto seemed happy to talk about the branch of the forces they were in, their comrades, where they'd been posted and what work they'd done since they were demobbed.

'Will we have any more singing?' another man asked. 'That really cheers me up. It can be lonely sometimes being old. My missus died a few years ago, and we didn't have any kiddies.'

My heart went out to him. He'd lived through so much and now was so low. 'Do you come here to the club often?' I asked.

'I can't walk that far. It's a pity I'd because I'd like to. It's good to see everyone. I hear they have some right good dos here. Today one of my neighbours gave me a lift, but he can't do that regularly.'

Bletchley Park was full of voluntary groups as well as different sports and entertainment ones. 'Leave it with me,' I said. 'Jot your name and address on some paper and give it to the man on the desk. I'll see if I can find someone who can give you a lift once a week. How does that sound?'

His face lit up. 'Would you? That would be marvellous.'

'I can't promise, but I'll see what I can do.' A bell let me know it was time to get ready for the second half. 'I'll have to go in a minute.'

'Before you go, I must say I love your Mother Goose, by the way. He makes a right good woman. Does the bloke who's playing her work at the Park?'

I smiled, remembering what George looked like in his normal clothes. He was one of the civvies at the Park, so never in uniform, but always very dapper. 'Yes, but I don't know what his job is.'

Carolyn, who'd organised the show but wasn't in it, was also socialising with the audience. Her smile and easy manner got a good response from the men she spoke to. I'd noticed that recently when she was watching the rehearsals or with us all in the Beer Hut, she didn't seem to look at George much, or seek him out. Then something else occurred to me. She looked a lot at Robert, the technical man in the show. And he looked at her, too. Yet I didn't see them talking to each other.

Was something going on between them?

Pushing that to the back of my mind, I went backstage and found Peggy there looking stunning in a dress that would have done Vera Lynn proud. It was cream, figure hugging, and off the shoulder. She wore high heels I'd never seen before. She looked like a film star. She'd already told me that someone at the Park had lent her the dress.

She was absolutely terrified. 'I can't do it! I can't sing!' she repeated over and over. I put my arms round her. 'I've heard you sing around Happy Days and in the pub. You're brilliant.' I pulled her by the arm. 'Come with me!'

I dragged her to a side room and while the audience was getting settled and the pianist was beginning to play, I got her to go through some voice-warming exercises. I'd never done them myself, but I'd seen someone do it when I was in a show with the ARP wardens.

Two minutes was enough to calm her, and I gave her another hug and pep talk, then walked back to the stage with her. Archie was ready to introduce her.

'So, welcome back to part two. I hope you enjoyed your refreshments. Before we continue with *Mother Goose*, I promised you a very special treat. And here she is – it's Peggy Kent. Come on now, give her a big round of applause!'

They certainly did. With her sexy dress, scarlet lipstick and perfect victory roll, she did a wiggle and waved to them in a flirtatious way. She not only got the men clapping, she got a lot of whistles and catcalls, too. She grinned and took several bows, and she hadn't even begun to sing.

Then, like a professional, she nodded to the pianist and began to sing a popular Billy Murray song, 'Sister Susie's Sewing Shirts for Soldiers'. It was quite a tongue twister, and we'd practised at Happy Days several times. Each time she sang the chorus, Bronwyn, and I stepped to the side of the stage holding a man's shirt and pretended to sew it. Our entrance lasted only a few seconds, but it got a laugh from the men who were already singing along.

The next song was 'Are We Downhearted', and every person there, including us backstage, shouted 'No!' in the chorus. The third was 'Goodbye-ee' and the final song was Vera Lynn's 'We'll Meet Again'.

Although everyone sang along, there wasn't a dry eye in the house. I sniffled and blew my nose, remembering the man I'd loved who died and the people who I'd seen die or injured in the Blitz. All the men, and several of the cast, would have lost someone dear to them and the song always plucked the heart strings.

I looked at Peggy from the wings and saw tears trickling down her cheeks, too. At the end of the song, the room was completely silent apart from one or two sobs and the sound of a man blowing his nose. Then the spell was broken, and the applause was thunderous.

She had a standing ovation, and the crowd kept calling her back. In case this happened, she and the pianist had chosen 'Don't Sit Under the Apple Tree'. It was a new song, but played on the radio such a lot she thought they'd know it. And it was a cheerful song to lead them into the second half of the panto.

It was an outstanding success. The cast, including me, all hammed it up, and the audience did us proud laughing, joining in, and generally enjoying themselves. When we'd all taken our final bow, with Peggy in the middle, we waved goodbye. We thought the men would never leave the hall. They were energised, lively and chatting to each other. A good number of them went into the bar next.

'You okay?' I asked Peggy as we changed from our stage clothes. 'That Vera Lynn song is a real tear-jerker, isn't it?'

She looked as if she might cry again. 'Tell you the truth, Lil, singing that song made me realise I made a mistake coming here. I thought being away from Linda was the sensible thing to do. And I 'ad that bloke for a while too. That was a mistake and no kidding. But now I've 'ad 'er with me, I can't let 'er go again.'

'But Marion...' I started.

She stepped out of her beautiful dress, folded it carefully in tissue paper, put it in a box and pulled on a jumper. 'It's all right. I won't take 'er from Marion. She never needs to know who I really am, but I'm moving back to be near 'er. I want to see 'er growing up. It'll be easy to get a barmaid's job. If not, I'll work in a factory or on the buses. Plenty of jobs in London. I'm going to give in my notice and leave the Park.'

14

I was thrilled when Carolyn invited me to London for the day with her. Her life was so different from mine, it was sure to be a day to remember. And better still, she offered to pay for any meals.

She wanted to see a show and didn't like going alone. All her friends, the 'people like her' were busy elsewhere, so my luck was in. She'd got tickets for a musical comedy *Let's Face It!*, with music by Cole Porter. Although I'd lived in London during the Blitz and occasionally had time and sometimes money to go to shows, it had been a while.

Even in its sorry bombed state, London still had a buzz. After sleepy Bletchley, there seemed to be an overwhelming number of people, buses, taxis and even horse and carts. Everyone seemed in a hurry, heads down, dashing here and there.

Carolyn had the day all planned out for us. Starting with tea in a posh hotel, then a lunchtime concert at the National Gallery, a visit Harrods, then the theatre.

I'd been to the Savoy before, for her big birthday party. It had been memorable because a bomb dropped on part of the hotel.

Last time I went there, the 'SAVOY' sign was half hanging off. Now it was proudly back in place. We walked through the elegant entrance hall with its startling black and white tiled floor, and into a room I hadn't been in before. It was the dining room. In the centre was a beautiful gazebo. 'See how it reflects the dome in the ceiling,' Carolyn said. 'Pity they had to cover the glass in case of bombing. It was stunning before.' Tables were set with cloths starched so much they could cut you and the cutlery shone so much you could put your make-up on with one.

Food at the Park was bad and our home-made meals using rations were not much better. The Savoy reminded me that some people lived very differently. We not only had a choice of teas – most of which I'd never heard of – but cakes, scones and pastries. Naughtily, I snuck one in my bag to give to Bronwyn when I got home.

'Oh look,' Carolyn said, trying not to be obvious. 'Isn't that Noël Coward over there? I must tell Mummy I've seen him. She'll be so jealous!'

It was. He was holding forth with three other people at the table while smoking a cigarette from a fancy holder.

Classical music was not my thing, and a couple of times poor Carolyn had to nudge me awake at the concert in the basement of the National Gallery. I was glad when it was over and we could go for lunch. Not that I had much room after all those cakes.

'Let's just grab a sandwich, darling,' Carolyn said. 'We'll have more time for shopping.'

So we headed for Harrods and had what she called a sandwich and what I'd call a full meal. In theory, no restaurant was supposed to charge more than five pounds for a dish, but they got round it by charging for 'extras'. In this case, it was the salad that came with the beef and mustard sandwich and the glass of champagne, which made me feel tiddly.

'How is Grant doing now?' Carolyn asked, inspecting her sandwich. 'Has he cheered up?'

'Not yet, I'm afraid. It's hard not to be impatient, but people say it can take ages to get back to normal after such a horrific injury.'

She wiped a crumb from her mouth with the massive starched napkin. 'You're very patient. I think in your position, I might have been tempted to have a bit of fun with someone else.'

She saw my shocked look.

'Oh, Lily, I don't mean go all the way, silly. Just go out for a meal or a drink. No harm in that. What with work and looking after Linda, our lives can be very dull. And if Grant found out, it might snap him out of whatever it is he's in.'

I was stunned at her suggestion, although if I was honest, some male company would be welcome. Bronwyn and I tended to go to everything together, but that wasn't always possible. She had her own life too. That increasingly included being with Thomas.

'How are things with George?' I asked, trying to change the subject.

She buttered half a teacake and loaded it with cream and jam. Luxuries we never saw in everyday life. 'Yes, George. I'm not sure where we're going, if I'm honest.'

Was this my opportunity to tell her my suspicions? I couldn't work out how to suggest anything. 'Aren't you close, then?'

'We're very good friends. We have a lot in common and Mummy would just love him for a son-in-law. He would certainly be able to keep me in comfort, but he's not...' She looked down at her plate.

'Not...?'

She went a gentle shade of pink. 'It's difficult. One gets so used to fighting off men, let's face it most of them only want one thing. I'm not sure George wants that at all.'

It took me a few seconds to take in what she was implying. 'So he's not very interested in the... intimate side of your relationship? Is that what you mean?' I asked.

She fiddled with her cutlery. 'Oh look, the waiter is bringing more tea. Let's talk about something else. Where shall we go shopping?'

No way could I afford any of the clothes shops Carolyn went into. I got bored watching her trying things on and having lengthy discussions about fabrics and fashions. As I waited, I pondered on our discussion over tea. It sounded as if I didn't need to tell Carolyn George's secret after all, and I was very relieved.

Finally, it was time for the theatre. We went into the Ladies' first and I was surprised how long she took putting on her make-up and doing her hair. She always looked great, but this was even better than normal. There was a real buzz in the auditorium and I overheard a couple of people saying they'd heard how good the show was.

I loved it. A hilarious story of misunderstandings and things going wrong with music you just had to tap your toes along with. As we left our seats, I felt high on the experience, the songs, the sounds and being with a big crowd somewhere luxurious after the small-town life in the Park and Bletchley itself. I hoped Carolyn had somewhere extra special for the last part of our day. A nightclub perhaps.

'Come on,' Carolyn said. 'I must freshen up before we go on.'

The Ladies' was full of women chatting, humming tunes from the show and generally saying how much they enjoyed the evening. As we refreshed our lipstick, I asked Carolyn where we were going next. She'd never mentioned it when she told me the plan for the day. She waved an arm in the air. 'Oh, we'll find somewhere fabulous. You wait and see.' Again, she spent ages making herself look gorgeous.

I soon found out why.

Since the war, the evening performances were earlier than they had been, so it wasn't late when we stepped onto the pavement outside the theatre. People were spilling out, saying goodbye to friends, looking for taxis and heading home or wherever they were going next.

Carolyn paused and looked around, and I wondered why we weren't leaving immediately.

'Oh look,' she cried, as if in great surprise. 'There's Robert from the Park. What a coincidence!' She began waving. 'Cooee! Cooee! Robert! Robert! We're here!'

I wasn't born yesterday. Even a baby would have seen through that charade.

Robert kissed us both on the cheeks. His cologne was strong enough to assault my nostrils. He had film star good looks and knew it.

'Fancy meeting you here! What a fluke!' he said, smoothing down his oiled hair. 'Carolyn, you look divine.' He paused. 'And you look lovely too, Lily. So good of you to keep Carolyn company. Why don't we all go for a drinkipoo?'

Carolyn put her arm through his. 'Darling, what a great idea! You'd like that too, wouldn't you, Lily? We'll find somewhere special to go.'

No way was I going to play gooseberry with those two. They'd be longing for me to go, anyway. Seeing them together upheld all my suspicions about them. And I knew he was married.

'I've got a bit of a headache, so I'll push off,' I said.

They didn't try to detain me, and as we separated I heard

Carolyn ask Robert, 'Where does your wife think you are tonight?'

* * *

'What's 'appened to Carolyn?' Peggy asked the next morning, coming downstairs with Linda. 'She didn't come 'ome last night. Weren't you in London with 'er yesterday?'

I wasn't surprised Carolyn hadn't returned. I'd have bet ten shillings Robert had a hotel all lined up for them under the names Mr and Mrs Smith. I could hardly tell Peggy that. 'After the show, she bumped into an old friend. She invited her to stay overnight. She's not on duty today, so who knows what time she'll appear.'

It was still dark outside, and I was getting ready for my eight o'clock shift. Peggy was due in a bit later.

'Are you still thinking of leaving and moving to be near Marion and Linda?' I asked as I put on my coat.

She was busy getting Linda ready for nursery. 'That's right. It's all decided. I've 'anded in my notice, so we leave on Christmas Eve. Soon! Oh my word, I've got so much to do before then! We're going to live with Mummy, aren't we, Linda?' She squeezed the little girl's hand.

'Live with Mummy! Live with Mummy!' the little girl chanted, jumping up and down. 'Will she 'ave that new baby yet?'

'Not yet. You'll 'ave to wait a bit longer.' She looked at me. 'I'm going to stay with Marion until a little while after the baby's born, then I'll find a place of me own. Somewhere near. Should work.'

I hugged her. 'It sounds like a great idea, but we are going to miss you so much.'

She looked at her watch. 'Oy, you'd better get going or you'll miss your bus.'

As I stood at the bus stop in the dark, I looked east and saw dawn was beginning to break. The sky in the other direction was still dark, but in the east subtle colours, yellow and red, were pushing aside the gloom. Shadows from power lines and buildings began to appear, and I hoped the day would soon warm up. Stamping my feet to try to stop the cold penetrating through my shoes, I saw the same dog as before looking for scraps. I only had a bit of stale bread to offer, but it was gobbled down in a second. I was glad that many people in Bletchley Town still had their pets. Pet owners across the country had been advised to put their pets down at the beginning of the war. The government leaflet said they'd use scarce food and be terrified during the bombing. I heard on the radio that three-quarters of a million pets were put down in just one week. All those lonely people, losing their much loved pets. It didn't bear thinking about.

There was a buzz around the corridors and canteen at the Park when I arrived. After the success of the panto with the war veterans, Archie decided we'd do our big performance on the afternoon of Christmas Eve in a church hall in the town. People in Bletchley always responded well to our shows, so I really looked forward to it.

Archie waylaid me in the canteen. 'I thought we'd also do carols on Christmas Day. Here. Cheer up everyone working when they'd rather be at home. Are you on duty, then?'

My face fell. I'd much rather have been at home with Mum or spending the day in front of the fire with Grant. 'Yes, eight till four. But I'd love to do carols after or even on my break.'

His face was alight with excitement. 'I don't think we need to be formal about it. Lots of people will be working so we can do the carols two or three times. Give everyone an opportunity to join in or just listen. Very informal. I'll put up notices. I've chosen really well-known carols, but I'll get the words printed just in case anyone doesn't know them. They'll have to share though, paper's too scarce to print loads. By the way, can you help decorate the tree when you've finished this afternoon if you've got time? It's already up in the billiard room.'

Decorating the tree gave me something to look forward to all day, taking my mind off the sometimes terrifying messages I heard from France. I popped into the billiard room in my midday break. The billiard tables had been moved over to the far wall and the tree, at least eight feet tall, stood proud, ready to be decorated. At Happy Days we'd decided not to get one. Bronwyn and I would be working Christmas Day, then she was going on to Thomas's house. Carolyn had managed to get some leave and was going back to her parents', and Peggy would be gone. But to keep Linda amused, we had made some paper chains with newspaper, using flour and water as glue. And we'd decorated some twigs from the garden, using pictures from magazines and some of my old lace bits that weren't big enough for anything practical. And I had some scraps of felt we turned into tiny Christmas trees. She could take them home to her mum.

When four o'clock came round, I was grateful to hand over my desk to the next girl and stretch my legs. I headed to the Beer Hut and had a cup of tea. Peggy was on duty and updated me with her plans. I offered to go with her and Linda all the way to Marion's because of the number of cases and bags they'd have. But when we checked the dates, I found I was on duty. But I could at least walk them to the station. 'Someone'll 'elp me,' she said cheerfully. 'I ain't worried.'

Handing back my used cup and saucer, I went over to the billiard room. Two girls, Maisie and Jenny, were already there, sorting through a couple of boxes of decorations. Many of them had seen better days, others needed to be dusted or wiped down. Between us, we agreed a colour scheme – red, white and blue. It seemed right to be patriotic. Jenny fetched a ladder, and we set about adorning the tree. It was a wonderfully relaxing thing to do after my shift, and I enjoyed being creative and getting to know the two girls better. As we worked, we sang some carols and the atmosphere was relaxed and hopeful.

'Let's hope next year brings an end to this war,' Maisie said when we stepped back to admire our work.

But none of us were sure that would happen.

* * *

By the time I got off the bus on the way home, I was feeling flat after the excitement of working with Maisie and Jenny on the tree. I'd already decided to make a cheese and potato pie for tea, enough for all of us. So I dragged myself into the kitchen, put on an apron and began peeling potatoes. As usual, I had to chip off a layer of dirt first and then wash them before I could even begin peeling them. I got out an onion, some milk, cheese, an egg and began work.

I thought I was in the house on my own, so I jumped when the kitchen door opened. It was Carolyn, looking more worse for wear than I'd ever seen her. Dark rings round her eyes and her usually glowing skin dull showed lack of sleep. It didn't take a genius to work out why.

'Hello, Lily,' she said, her voice sounding like she smoked heavily. 'I'm beat. I didn't get much sleep last night.'

'Sit down. I'll make you a cuppa,' I said, patting her shoulder. 'It's the least I can do after the lovely day you gave me yesterday. I don't think I thanked you for it properly, but I loved it.'

She squirmed. 'I'm sorry we left you like that after the show. I hope you got home okay.'

'It was much as usual.' I wanted to ask how her night went, but she probably wouldn't want to say, and I certainly didn't want any details. While the kettle boiled, I went back to preparing the veg, chopping the potatoes, onion and carrots into even-sized chunks.

I sat beside her when I'd made the tea, but she wasn't in a talkative mood beyond what we'd done the day before and the dress she'd bought.

'I'll go and have a bath,' she said wearily. 'I'll feel better then.'

I heard her run the bath, and ten minutes later get out. Only being allowed five inches of water didn't encourage a long soak, however tired you felt.

Then there was a knock on the door.

We didn't get many visitors, and Mrs W. never bothered to knock. It was probably someone collecting for old soldiers or something, I thought as I walked down the hall.

But it wasn't.

It was a heavily pregnant woman, and she looked furious. 'I want to see Carolyn,' she snarled.

Taken aback, my mouth refused to work immediately. 'Um, Carolyn. She's upstairs. It may not be convenient at the moment.'

She pushed past me and stood in the hall, clutching her stomach and leaning against a wall for support. 'I know you're not Carolyn. You're not his type. Go and fetch her. I'll wait all night if I have to.'

My nerves on edge, I asked her name.

'Mrs Williams. Mrs Robert Williams.'

The penny dropped. This was Robert's wife, and she looks as if she'd collapse any second. Or burst with rage.

'I think you'd better come into the living room while I get

her,' I said, opening the door for her. Before going upstairs, I nipped into the kitchen and fetched a glass of water, which I took to Mrs Williams. 'I'll get her now.'

The poor woman had sunk into a chair and looked done in, but she waved me away, so I headed for the stairs.

I knocked on Carolyn's door and went in without waiting for a reply. She was only wearing undies and was smoothing cream on her legs. Surprised, she looked up. 'What is it? You look like you've had a fright.'

'It's Mrs Williams, Robert's wife. She's downstairs demanding to see you.'

The colour left her face, and she dropped her pot of cream. Some slid out of the pot onto the thin carpet.

'Oh my word, what'll I do?' She paused. 'I know. Tell her it's not convenient. I'm ill.' For a second she looked relieved, thinking she's solved the problem.

'That won't wear. She says she'll wait all night if necessary. And she's looking good and mad.'

Carolyn fell back on the bed. 'What am I going to do? Robert assured me she doesn't know about us.'

I sat on a chair near her. 'You'll have to go down and face the music. I don't think you have a choice.'

With a heavy sigh, she got up and began putting on her clothes. Her movements were so slow it was as if she had had a stroke. 'Will you stay in the room with us, Lily? Please? I don't think I can face her on my own.'

'I'll stay if you want me to, but don't expect me to say anything.'

Despite the waiting woman, she stopped to brush her hair and put on bright lipstick. 'Warpaint!' she muttered as she headed for the stairs.

At the door, I saw her take a deep breath before turning the handle. 'Mrs Williams?' she said as she took a step in. 'I'm Carolyn. I understand you want to see me.'

Mrs Williams struggled out of her chair, her advanced pregnancy making her clumsy. 'So you're her. Robert's latest bit on the side. I wanted to see what you looked like.'

Carolyn gasped and clutched the door handle as if it would stop her from falling. 'I... I...' she stuttered.

'What? You didn't know he was married? Don't give me that. I've got friends up at the Park, you know. I've been hearing what's been going on. And I don't know where he was last night, but I'm damn sure it wasn't staying with an old army colleague like he said.'

She turned to me. 'Was she here all last night?'

My face burned, but I refused to answer. It was enough for her.

'Well,' she said, turning back to Carolyn. 'I don't know if he's done the whole "My wife and I never have sex routine" with you. He usually uses that with his trollops. As you can see—' she patted her stomach '—it's not true. And don't think you're the first or even the second trollop. In fact, I'm pretty sure you're not even the only one at the moment.'

Carolyn's head jerked back, and she fell into the nearest chair. 'I'm... sorry...' she said. 'I never...'

Mrs Williams picked up her bag. 'I dare say he's lied to you as much as he's lied to me. But I'm here to tell you that if you don't stop seeing him, I will sue for divorce and you will be named as a co-respondent. Your name will be in all the papers.'

And lifting her head high, she walked out of the door and into the hall. I opened the front door for her and she disappeared into the gloom.

I went back into the living room and Carolyn sat as if in a daze. I went back into the kitchen and found the half bottle of port we'd hidden from Mrs W. Grabbing two glasses, I went back to the living room. She was sitting with her head in her hands.

'Here, have this,' I said, handing her a glass.

She took a gulp and almost choked.

'Want to talk about it?' I asked.

She shook her head, but spoke anyway. 'He told me they were separated but still shared a house. He promised he was leaving her, getting a divorce so we could get married. And he certainly never told me she was pregnant.'

I felt so sad for her. She'd been so thoroughly hoodwinked by this man. 'I know it's a shock for you, but I couldn't help feeling sorry for her too. Almost ready to give birth and married to a bounder. You're better off without him, Carolyn.'

She looked into her glass. 'But how can I give him up? I still love him, Lily.'

The front door opened and Peggy came in with Linda. 'Just putting Linda to bed!' she called.

'You know,' I said, 'I used to have a friend who went out with married men.' I didn't say I was talking about Bronwyn – that was in her past. 'She loved the excitement of the chase and the illicit sex, much more than she loved the men. Or so she told me.'

Carolyn didn't respond immediately, but instead poured herself another glass of port, drinking it in one go. 'I'm sorry, Lily, I need to be alone. I'm going to bed and I won't want any dinner. I'll see you in the morning.'

Feeling the weight of both women's pain pulling me down, I went back into the kitchen. I put the veg on to cook and grated the cheese, my movements ponderous.

'What's up with Carolyn?' Peggy said when she came down ten minutes later. 'I just saw 'er going into the bathroom and she looked like death.'

'It's a long story,' I said.

But I wasn't going to tell her.

15

Christmas was just a few days away, and I still had to buy some things. Bronwyn and I would both be on eight till four duty. We'd probably go to the Beer Hut afterwards, but would want a meal when we got home that evening.

The shops were doing their best to look festive, but it was a poor show. There were signs outside the post office urging us to post letters before 20 December. On the wall inside was another poster with a drawing of Father Christmas and the words 'Make it a war Savings Christmas!'

Each year of the war made it more difficult to celebrate Christmas as we'd want to. Everything was scarce, and I was glad someone at the Park had given me a couple of second-hand toys in good condition that I could give to Linda. Paper was in such short supply that shopkeepers were forbidden to wrap anything except when they delivered. So I had to remember to take a bag, especially if I was buying meat or even Christmas presents.

I'd spent ages trying to decide what to give everyone. There was so little in the shops and I didn't have much money. But my sewing skills saved the day again. I had plenty of bits of material and even some whole second-hand clothes I'd got at various jumble sales and not altered yet.

I made Linda a Christmas stocking and put a dress for her doll in it. They wouldn't be too bulky or heavy to carry home to her mum's. Bronwyn was getting a short jacket made from a man's coat. Peggy, a straight skirt made from a flared one that had a small tear. Carolyn was the hardest. She had plenty of money to buy new clothes when she had enough coupons. After much dithering and hunting for ingredients, I decided to make her some honeycomb toffee. I'd kept a pretty glass jar and would tie some ribbon round the top. I was glad we didn't always work the same shifts or it would have been impossible to do all this in secret.

So one evening, three days before Christmas, I was out in the cold trying to find some buttons for Peggy's skirt and a few other things. As I passed houses, I could hear Christmas carols being played on the radio. Despite the chill, people were cheery as we passed each other.

I'd just found the buttons when I bumped into Douglas, one of the men at the Park. We worked in the same hut, but not in the same room, so rarely got to talk to each other. I had no idea what his job was.

'Lily!' he said. 'Nice to see you. I'm just going for a pint. Do you fancy coming with me? Have you got time?'

I thought about what Carolyn had said about having dates because of Grant's continuing distance. I'd decided not to take her advice. Shell shock like his could take a long time to disappear, and it was far too soon to give up on him. But this wasn't a date, was it? It was just having a drink with someone from work. No romantic expectations and I wouldn't feel disloyal.

'I'd love one,' I said. 'I've just finished my shopping.'

The Duck and Drake was nearest and we could hear laughter from inside. 'This sounds lively. Shall we give it a try?' he asked.

The pub hadn't been open long, but it was already full. Old ladies sat by the fire as usual, small groups of men leaned on the bar talking about the latest war news. American and Australian troops had finally pushed the Japanese out of Burma.

'What can I get you?' Douglas asked.

'Half of cider please.' As he pushed his way to the bar, I found a small table vacant and sat down. After queueing in the cold outside every shop, I was pleased to rest my feet in the warm. I'd never taken much notice of Douglas before. We simply passed each other in the corridor sometimes. He rarely acknowledged me. He was short, probably about five foot six inches, and a bit plump. His hair was so short it was almost shaven.

He soon returned with our drinks and pushed his chair a little nearer to mine. 'There you are, dear. Hope you like it. I waved my ten bob note at the barmaid and she served me first.'

I'd watched him. He didn't just wave the note, he'd nudged other men out of the way too. It was a sign of what was to come.

'How are you liking your job?' he asked, looking at me searchingly.

But he didn't wait for a reply. 'I love my work. I can't talk about it, of course, but it is fascinating and some people say I'm one of the leading experts in the field. Of course, it's not all down to me. I work with a great bunch of chaps, salt of the earth. We have one girlie in the team, too. She's surprisingly bright.' What was surprising was how long someone could talk about their job without actually telling you what it was.

And bore you to death in the process. But I was left in no doubt that whatever it was, he was very important for its success. I wondered if his colleagues would agree.

Okay, I thought, I won't be staying long enough for a second cider. I soon learned he could have bored for England. His hobbies, his wealth, his previous job – well paid and prestigious, of course. Then it was ten minutes about his favourite route to Scotland.

I switched off and let him talk. Looking around was much more interesting. A couple were holding hands at a nearby table and whispering sweet nothings to each other. The old ladies were knitting what looked like very long striped scarves. Two very old men without a tooth between them played dominoes.

The warmth of the bar after the cold outside lulled me into a sort of daze. Douglas droned on beside me, too busy talking about himself to realise I was taking not a bit of notice.

But I came round with a jolt when I looked through the bar to the snug. The door had opened a crack and inside, I could hardly believe my eyes, was Robert. He had his arm round a pretty young woman who was gazing at him adoringly. She wasn't Carolyn, and she wasn't his wife.

What an absolute bounder he was.

I was tempted to go and tell her not to trust him, that he was a serial philanderer. The trouble was, he'd just deny it and if she was as enamoured of him as she looked, she'd believe him, not me. I felt sorry for her, knowing the heartache she'd soon be experiencing.

His wife hadn't been wrong about him having more than one woman on the side. I wondered if she'd stay with him. That baby must be due any day, so it wasn't a good time for her to think about leaving him. I wondered if they already had any children and what their everyday life was like.

Should I tell Carolyn? I pondered on it while Douglas bleated on endlessly about his favourite cars. 'Everyone so admired that car. Pity about petrol rationing, I can't get to use it as often as I'd like. I love to head off to the coast or into town to see a show. Still, after the war I'll get a new one.'

A barmaid walked around collecting empties, and accidentally nudged his arm, spilling a minuscule amount of beer on his sleeve. He stood up and made a huge fuss of brushing it off. 'Can't you be more careful!' he snarled at her. Then, without pause, carried on talking about his car.

I thought about my time with Grant. I'd never been bored like I was with Douglas, and he'd never been rude to staff like that either. Making the comparison made me miss him all over again.

Archie had told me he'd gone to London for a small operation on his leg. He'd be back the next day, but Archie didn't know if he'd be at work. I decided if I didn't see him at the Park, I'd put a letter through his door. The thought of Christmas without him punctured my heart.

Then I was brought back to the moment. Douglas put his clammy hand on my knee. I was so taken aback, I just knocked it off without thinking and stood up. He looked surprised. It was undoubtedly news to him that he wasn't considered a good catch.

'Right, I've got lots to do. Thanks for the cider,' I said. He watched me put on my coat, his mouth flapping. I picked up my stuff and left without a backward glance.

At home Carolyn was in, sitting in the living room reading a book. I put away my shopping, then joined her. 'Carolyn, I've just seen something I need to tell you about. I'm afraid you won't like it.'

She put a bookmark in her book and looked at me. 'That sounds ominous. What is it?'

I gulped. 'I was just in the Duck and Drake. You know there's a snug in there? Well... I... saw Robert in there.' I could see her face beginning to change, and her shoulders drop. 'He was with another woman. He had his arm round her shoulders.'

She leaned back on the sofa. 'So his wife was right. I wasn't the only one. What a total bastard. How could I have been so blinded to what he was like?'

I moved to sit next to her and put my hand on her arm. 'Don't be hard on yourself. We all make mistakes. I know I have.'

'You? You always seem so sensible.'

I laughed. 'Well, not always. I went out with a lad who turned out to be a bad one. And when I finished with him, he just wouldn't leave me alone. Kept following me, giving me presents, generally making a right nuisance of himself.'

I hoped my story would take her mind off Robert's treachery.

Her eyes grew wide. 'I've never heard of such a thing. How did you get rid of him?'

'He gave me some presents he'd stolen. The police saw them and he ended up in jail. I don't know what I'd have done if that hadn't happened.'

She shook her head and gave a bitter laugh. 'I wish I could get Robert locked away. I bet his wife does, too.'

16

Christmas was ever nearer. I'd sent Mum a card and made presents for Carolyn, Bronwyn, Peggy and Linda, and that was all I needed to do. It felt very strange. At home or even while at Happy Days, I'd have been worrying about how to find suitable food to make a half-decent Christmas dinner. But Bronwyn had shed a shift so she could do midnight to eight. Then she planned to sleep for a few hours before spending the day with Thomas and his daughter.

I would still work eight till four that day and would be eating a no doubt awful apology for a Christmas dinner at the Park. I hoped there would be no cockroaches or mice in it.

But that wasn't the main thing on my mind. Peggy and Linda were leaving in two days, Christmas Eve, and we would miss them so much. Peggy was always good fun with her great sense of humour and her very direct way of speaking. I'd grown fond of little Linda, too. She'd had the plaster removed from her arm and was looking forward to showing off her now good arm to her mum. Peggy had one last day at the Beer Hut, then they'd be off the next morning, just in time to join Marion for Christmas.

As I went upstairs, I saw they were packing. Their door was open, so I joined them.

'Do you think Mummy will like this cardigan Bronwyn made for the baby?' Linda asked, inspecting it with a frown on her pretty forehead.

'She'll love it,' Peggy said. 'Let's pack it in between some clothes to keep it nice and clean.'

I perched on the end of the bed. 'So you're really leaving us? Can I help?'

Peggy smiled at me. 'You can 'elp keep madam amused while I get on with this.' She handed me a simple jigsaw, so I got on the floor and began helping Linda do it. She got impatient and tried to slam the pieces in with her palm if they didn't fit the first time. She was full of questions. 'Will the baby be a baby boy or a baby girl?' 'When can I play with it?' 'Will you 'ave some sweeties to give me for the train?'

Eventually, she slowed down, and it was her bedtime. Peggy put the half-filled cases away and told Linda to get ready for bed.

I left them to it and went out of the room. To my surprise, Carolyn was in her room, also packing. I hadn't heard her come in.

'Are you leaving in the morning?' I asked.

She was folding up some beautiful silk stockings. 'Yes, I'm getting an early train. I'll be glad to get away from the Park for a while. I'll especially be glad to get away from Robert.'

'Have you seen him, then?' I thought how awful it was to keep bumping into someone you still cared for, but also hated.

She sat on her bed, sighed, and folded her arms. 'You wouldn't believe his cheek. He sought me out on my way to the canteen. I tried to shake him off, but he wouldn't go.'

'What did he want? Not another date, surely?'

She gave a hollow laugh. 'That's exactly what he wanted. His wife must have told him she'd been round to see me. Did he care? He did not. "But, darling," he kept saying, "we're so good together."'

It was easy to imagine. He was a smoothy who thought he was irresistible. 'Blimey, Carolyn, what did you do?'

A wide grin lit up her face and her eyes sparkled. 'I turned to him and gave him a big smile. He thought he'd won me round, but he was wrong. I did something I never thought I'd ever do. I kneed him very hard in the you-know-whats.'

I gasped. 'You didn't!'

'I certainly did, and I didn't give a damn that there were people around. Not many, but some must have seen. He doubled over and almost fell to the floor, calling me all the names under the sun. I spat on him and strode off to get my meal. I didn't look back.'

I was astounded. 'Wow, Carolyn. I can't imagine you spitting, much less kneeing someone. That's a side of you I've never seen before.'

She ran her fingers through her hair. 'I have to say, it felt good. Powerful. I'm rather proud of myself. I don't think he'll be bothering me again! If I kneed him hard enough, he won't be bothering anyone else for a while either.'

I tried not to feel envious of the beautiful underwear she was packing as we talked. 'And what about George? You weren't sure about him the last time we spoke.'

She stood up and began packing again. This time it was a royal blue satin nightdress with cream lace. 'He's not for me. Mummy might like him for a son-in-law, but I don't want a relationship without... passion. I've told him. We'll still be friends, but that's all. Who knows, perhaps I'll meet someone at the Christmas parties at home who'll take my mind off both of them.'

17

It was Peggy's last day at the Beer Hut and she decided to go out in style. Instead of her usual attractive, but sensible, outfits, she wore a figure-hugging black skirt, a low-cut white blouse and some red tinsel in her hair. She'd asked me to go in my midday break, and I wouldn't have missed it for the world.

Two other barmaids were on duty, and it was obvious they were doing all the work so she could enjoy her final day. One saw me come in and nudged Peggy, knowing we were friends. She came rushing over, dodging round the larger than usual number of customers.

'You came!' she said, giving me a big hug. 'The girls say they've got something special lined up for me. They were waiting for you to come so they can do whatever it is.' She grabbed my hand and pulled me towards the bar. The room immediately hushed and everyone looked at her.

Jane, one of her colleagues, stood on a chair. 'As you all know,' she shouted, 'our favourite barmaid, Peggy, is leaving today. What will we all do without her? She's kept us entertained with stories of her life in London and more jokes than we can count. And there's her singing, of course.' She turned to Peggy. 'We are so sorry to see you go and have a little something for you.'

The third barmaid handed her a small cardboard box. It seemed heavy. 'We spent ages wondering what to buy you. But then we remembered you'll have to carry whatever it was to London. So we decided to give you the money. Everyone contributed. It won't make you rich, but it'll help keep you afloat for a few days when you arrive.' She looked at the customers. 'Come on now, everyone – HIP HIP HOORAY!'

The noise they made was probably heard from the big house. It was so joyous.

Peggy went bright red, and her smile was a mile wide. 'I don't know what to say, but thank you all. Thank you so much. I've enjoyed serving every one of you, and I promise to keep all your secrets to myself!'

This got a good laugh, then shouts of 'SPEECH! SPEECH!'

'I'm no good at speeches. 'Ow about I sing you a song instead. I bet you all like Andrews Sisters' numbers.'

And with that, she moved all the glasses off the bar, gave it a wipe, dried it, and climbed on to it. Jane pretended to do a drum roll by tapping on the bar. One of the customers produced a mouth organ for backing, and Peggy gave a rousing version of 'Boogie Woogie Bugle Boy'. She did all the gestures, including pretending to play the bugle. One couple started dancing, and many people sang along. When she'd finished, there were calls for an encore.

'Only one more song or I'll fall off this bar with all the drinks you lot 'ave been buying me.' She grinned and did a deep bow. 'So how about "Don't Sit Under the Apple Tree with Anyone Else But Me"?' She got whistles and catcalls in reply. The harmonica player led her in and she swayed and sang as if she were on a stage, not on the bar in the Beer Hut. There were more calls for

an extra song, but instead she shouted, 'Let's 'ave a sing-song.'
After a little hesitation, she started singing 'Let the People Sing'
and other well-known show songs. It went on for more than half
an hour and it seemed as if the applause would never end.

She bowed and curtsied. 'No more now, but thank you all for
your applause. It's been an 'onour and a privilege to serve you all.
God bless!'

* * *

'What's 'appened? Why can't I see?' Linda asked as we stepped
outside the door early the next morning.

'It's fog, sweet'eart,' Peggy told her.

'What's fog?'

Peggy looked at me as if I would know the answer. I had no
idea how to explain it or what caused it. 'Ask your teacher when
you start at big school.'

The fog was thick, much thicker than that evening when I
saw George holding hands with another man. The hazy greyness
and curls of smoky air currents made it difficult to judge
distances or even tell where pavements ended and road began. I
felt as if we were in a dream world, cut away from reality. Sounds
were softened by the fog too, making it difficult to identify them
and tell where they came from.

'It doesn't look like it'll be a white Christmas,' Peggy said.
'Pity. Linda would've enjoyed playing in the snow.'

We plodded along, trying to hold Linda between us, but also
holding their cases and bags. 'I 'ope a bus comes along soon,'
Peggy said as we reached the bus stop. 'This fog gets right into
your bones, don't it!'

'Should be here in five minutes,' someone said. The fog was
so thick we'd hardly been aware there was anyone nearby.

We struggled onto the bus when it arrived, ten minutes late. The conductor helped us on with our luggage. 'Leaving the country, are you?' she said with a cheeky grin.

The bus was full of smells of damp clothes and cigarette smoke and I longed for some fresh air. But the weather forecast said fog for three days, all over Christmas. No fresh air for a while.

'Will you look for a job straight away?' I asked once we'd settled into our seats.

'Nah. That money they gave me last night at the Beer 'Ut, God bless 'em, will see me over until a couple of weeks after the nipper comes if I'm careful. Then I'll 'ave to look.'

I looked out of the window, trying to judge when to ring the bell to get off, but the fog obscured everything. It was like living on a strange, white planet. Occasionally something would pass close by the bus, making us jump – a horse and cart, a coal lorry, another bus going in the opposite direction.

'Station stop!' shouted the kind conductor who'd called the name of every stop. We struggled off with our bags and cases, Linda clinging on to our arms.

The fog swirled as we stepped off the bus leaving just enough for us to see which direction the pavement was, then it closed in again.

We hadn't gone ten steps when something terrible happened.

A horse, no doubt lost in the fog, jumped onto the pavement in front of us, dragging its cart with it. With an enormous noise, screeching and dragging, the cart turned over, and the driver was flung at our feet. The horse stopped, neighing, its eyes wide with fear.

'I'm frightened!' Linda cried, clinging on to Peggy's skirts. 'Horsey!'

Swearing loudly, the cart driver picked himself up, brushed

himself down, and went to the horse. 'You stupid animal,' he said, but his tone was gentle.

'Excuse me, ladies, I need to get this sorted out. You'd probably best go on ahead. It'll take a while.'

Cautiously, we stepped into the road to get round the cart and almost got run over by a car. Linda cried again as the driver sounded his horn. It had to be the most stressful walk I'd had in Bletchley, but nothing compared to walking in London during the Blitz.

Finally, I got my penny platform ticket and went with Peggy and Linda to the right platform. If the train was on time, we just had five minutes to wait.

'You've bin ever so good,' Peggy said. 'I'll never forget being 'ere with you and the others. The Beer 'Ut too.'

I grasped her hand. 'We'll never forget you, Peggy.'

'Nor me!' Linda demanded. 'Don't forget me neither!'

I bent and kissed her. 'I won't. I'll remember you for always.'

We heard the sound of the train in the distance, muffled by the fog but still recognisable. 'What's 'appening about Grant?' Peggy said. 'Quick, tell me before the train comes.'

'Archie tells me he'll be back from the hospital in London today. That's all I know. I'll just have to take every day as it comes.'

'Tell you what. I'll send you a postcard when the nipper arrives, and you send me one when 'e comes to 'is senses. Is it a deal?'

The smoke from the train combined with the fog made it hard to see and harder still to breathe properly. I hugged them both. 'Have a lovely life,' I whispered.

A soldier helped them on with their luggage and they were soon lost from sight.

Sad, but happy for their new life, I left the station. Time was catching up with me and I looked for a bus to take me home. I had a day's leave because of the panto and had to get ready and remind myself of my lines.

* * *

As I sat having my tea and toast, a second breakfast after leaving Peggy and Linda, I wondered if Grant would get in touch. If he'd had another operation on his leg, he might still be feeling poorly. Surely, though, he could send me a message.

Mrs W. came in as I was washing up. 'Bit quiet around here,' she said, flicking ash from her cigarette in an ashtray. 'I'll have to think about getting someone for Peggy's room now she's gone. In the new year perhaps. There's always plenty of people looking for rooms. How're you doing? You look a bit down in the dumps.'

I put on a smile for her benefit. 'Just a bit tired after seeing Peggy and Linda off. It's our panto today at the church hall. Are you coming? It's bound to be good. Some children from the school will be doing a song.'

She pulled a face. 'Pantos aren't really my thing, but I'll think about it. It's just you and Bronwyn in it, isn't it?'

'That's right. It's *Mother Goose*. She's the fairy, and I'm Mary Quite Contrary.'

She laughed and got out another cigarette. 'We could all do with a golden egg or two, I reckon.' She looked at the big clock. 'Anyway, I'd better get going, lots to do today. Good luck with the show.'

* * *

On my way to the hall, I called into the school. Enid, the teacher who had helped with the Halloween party, had organised a group of children to sing a song as part of the panto. They were to sing 'Cackle, Cackle Mother Goose', a song I'd never heard before. They weren't allowed at the Park, and she had rehearsed them at school.

'All okay for this afternoon?' I asked when I caught up with her on a break.

'They're very excited, even the ones who are usually shy. It's a great opportunity for them.' She held up her hands. 'I know what you're going to say. Yes, we'll have them there in good time.'

We'd decided they should also see the panto. This meant them coming in earlier so they could see where they had to stand. But until it was their turn, they could sit and enjoy the show.

As I left, I saw Bella in the playground, Thomas's daughter. She smiled and waved to me. She would be one of the choir singing in the show.

I got to the church hall a couple of hours before the panto doors opened. Bronwyn arrived a few minutes after me. Archie was already busy seeing to the set, moving furniture and the backing sheet. Bronwyn and I helped the caretaker put out the chairs. A lot of tickets had been sold, so we should have a full house. Proceeds were to go to the school.

'Did Peggy get off okay?' Bronwyn asked. 'It's a pity she can't sing like she did for the veterans. Still, we'll have the school choir. People always love them.'

As time moved on, backstage filled with performers getting ready. There was an electric atmosphere amongst us. It might only be a church hall, but we were as nervous as if it had been the West End in London. The men were messing about, joking, trying to reassure themselves. A couple had already been on the beer from the smell of them.

Bronwyn slid into the lovely evening dress Mrs W. had loaned her. The colour complemented her colouring perfectly. Archie spotted her and wolf-whistled. She grinned and did a twirl, then stepped back. Straight onto her wings. 'Oh no!' she cried, holding them up. 'They're bent out of shape and torn. I can't go on with them like that.'

Archie stepped forward. 'Come here, my lovely. I always bring a small toolkit with me for such emergencies.' He had the wings straightened within five minutes, and then he handed them to me. 'I'd bet a penny to a pound you've got a needle and thread in your bag, Lily.'

I had a very basic one, but the colour thread would do. Bronwyn helped to put up my hair as I sewed. 'Let's hope that's the only mishap we have,' I said. 'By the way, I saw Bella at the school. I suppose it must be going well with her if you're spending tomorrow with them.'

She smiled. 'It seems a long slog. With her mum dying when she was born, she's not used to another woman in the house. She might be little, but she feels like she is the woman in the house. Can't blame her. There's still a long way to go.'

I looked at her in the mirror. 'Are you moving in with them, then? Has he proposed?'

She play slapped my shoulder. 'Of course not. We've hardly known each other for five minutes. Don't worry, *cariad*, I'm not about to leave Happy Days.'

As the time of the performance drew near, the dressing area filled up to the point of crowded. It smelled of hot bodies, make-up, beer and panic.

I was buttoning my top when Archie came over, looking flustered. 'I'm so sorry, Lily, I forgot to tell you. I called in on Grant earlier. He's a bit done in after his op, but he hoped to be well enough to be out and about tomorrow. He asked me to tell you.'

'There,' said Bronwyn. 'Man's come to his senses. That's lush, that is.'

The butterflies in my stomach at the news drove all my lines out of my head. 'Oh my goodness, Bronwyn, my brain's turned to mush. I can't remember what I'm supposed to be doing.'

She bent down so she was level with my face. 'It's like this, see, you've just got to control your breathing. Now follow me, breathe in and out slowly.'

It worked. Less than two minutes later, I'd calmed down enough to think. But I was still worried. It was wonderful that Grant had sent the message, but I still couldn't be sure how he'd be. If he was still in love with me, surely he'd have got in touch direct. What if he was as remote as before or even wanted to break it off?

Bronwyn handed me a cracked cup 'There, get that inside you, girl. It's an inch of port I found in the cupboard. I can see that mind of yours going round in circles. Go on, drink it.'

I took a big gulp and the smooth liquid warmed my body and slowed my mind. 'You're right, thanks, Bron. But I've still got to check my lines!'

We could hear the audience coming in, chairs scraping on the floor, people chattering. Archie went round to speak to each of us, giving us a pep talk and making sure we were okay. Enid popped her head in to say the children had arrived. The pianist started to play some cheerful music to keep the audience amused while they waited for the start.

'Right, everybody in place!' Archie called, and the music changed. The butterflies in my stomach went on a rampage. Instead of Archie introducing the show, George in his full Mother Goose outfit and make-up, stepped between the maroon curtains.

I watched him from the wings. He crossed his arms under his well-padded bosom and looked around sternly until the audience was quiet. Then he wagged his finger at them like a teacher telling them off.

'Right, you lot, I've heard a lot about you and I want no trouble from any of you. Especially the grown-ups! I know what you're like.' He wagged his finger again. That got a giggle from the children. 'We're about to start the show but I wanted to remind you that this show is in aid of school funds. There will be people at the back when you leave with buckets. If you can spare any pennies, or better still shillings, or better still notes, they'll all be for a good cause. Now. Are you going to behave?'

He cupped his hand to his ear and looked around.

'I SAID, ARE YOU GOING TO BEHAVE?'

A few people in the audience had been primed and shouted out 'OH, NO, WE'RE NOT!'

George turned to step back behind the curtains, and a pair of gigantic pink knickers fell to the floor from under his skirt. He held them up and pretended to be confused about them, then threw them at the pianist.

The audience howled. It was a great stunt.

He disappeared back behind the curtains, the pianist started, the curtains opened and we were off!

I only forgot my lines once, and the prompter rescued me before anyone noticed. As before when I'd been on stage, my initial terror soon disappeared, and I loved what I was doing.

The 'horse' paused at one stage and there was a deafening fart. I hoped it was a stage one. But as in rehearsals, the rear legs detached themselves and the actor looked at the audience waving away the smell. 'That is just plain disgusting, isn't it, kids? I think I'll kick his backside.' He paused and looked at the front half where the actor was hamming it up, swinging one leg around.

'Oh, now why can't I kick his backside?' He turned around

three times and his tail swung behind him. 'Oh no! I AM THE BACKSIDE!'

He clowned around, pretending to try to kick himself in the backside. Then he went to the head of the horse and shouted, 'I'M NOT GETTING BACK IN THERE IF YOU DO THAT AGAIN!'

Amid gales of laughter, both halves left the stage.

Jack-be-nimble came on riding a child's bicycle, his knees knocking his chin. He said his line and swiftly rode off again.

And in what seemed no time at all it was the interval. The children in the choir left their seats. They were singing first in the second half and did everyone proud. Despite it being a funny song there were one or two damp eyes in the audience.

Bronwyn made a fantastic fairy, the disaster with her wings forgotten. Bella stroked her dress during the interval when we were having a cuppa. 'I wish I had a dress like that,' she said. Bronwyn bent down and whispered. 'I'll let you into a secret, it's not mine. I borrowed it.'

Bella looked impressed. 'Can I borrow it?'

Another whisper. 'I'll let you try it on tomorrow, but I'll have to take it home with me.'

Usually Archie came on stage to say the last few words after the show. This time, though, he spontaneously got George to do it because he'd been so popular.

There were cheers as soon as he walked through the curtains. He held up his hands. 'Thank you, ladies and gentlemen, and children, too. I hope you've enjoyed the show as much as we've enjoyed performing it. And, of course, a special thank you to our young choir.' He led the applause for them.

'Just a reminder that there will be buckets at the back as you leave. If you can spare a little money, it will all go to a good cause.' He hitched his bosom up again. 'Do you know, that pianist bloke never gave me back my unmentionables. Isn't that a disgrace?'

Cries of 'YES, IT IS!'

'So I got a new pair.' He lifted up his skirt and displayed a massive blue pair that came down past his knees.

The applause raised the roof, and we took three curtain calls. The children, who had gone back to watch the rest of the second half, stood up and were applauded too.

With my limited experience of being on stage, I'd learned that the moment the curtains closed for the last time, all energy vanished. It was as if it left with the audience. Christmas Eve was no different. Archie came backstage to congratulate us as we took off our make-up and got changed. He took time to have a word with each of us individually, which certainly made me feel special. It recharged my energy too.

I helped move and stack the chairs. Someone else swept the floor and stage.

'Right, my trusty actors. It's too early for the pub, but I had a word with the landlord at the Duck and Drake and if we go to the back door, he'll let us in.'

We were all so high that as soon as we had a drink, we began singing songs from the show. Jack-be-nimble was anything but and fell over after two drinks. Adrenaline kept us going long after the pub officially opened, and we were joined by members of the public.

It was still foggy when Bronwyn and I walked home, arm in arm for safety.

'So you'll see Grant tomorrow then, *cariad*?' she asked. 'Are you nervous?'

We almost bumped into a man walking his dog and blamed the fog, not the drink.

Surely Grant wouldn't dump me on Christmas Day, I told

myself but that didn't stop an empty feeling in the bottom of my stomach.

* * *

No lie-in on Christmas Day for me. I crept out of bed as quietly as I could, taking everything with me so I wouldn't disturb Bronwyn. I shivered as I put on my old woollen dressing gown, and tiptoed into the bathroom. With Peggy gone and Carolyn away, I felt okay about leaving my clothes in there until later.

I went down the stairs missing the one that creaked, but I needn't have bothered.

'I'm awake!' Bronwyn called. 'Make a cuppa for me!'

She came down in her dressing gown. 'I haven't wrapped Bella's present yet.'

'I've got a bit of last year's paper still. It's a bit crumpled but you can iron it.' I hurried upstairs to get it, aware I had to be at work at eight.

When I got back the iron was already heating up. Bronwyn put a towel on the table and got to work. 'I hope today goes well. We had something upsetting yesterday. A message I took had the code word spelled correctly.'

My heart sank. The Special Operations Executives radio operators used that as a way to let us know they had been compromised. The Germans would capture them, take over their radios and send us false messages. But they always corrected the spelling. Being captured meant torture and certain death. It was hard to imagine anything worse.

'Sorry,' Bronwyn said. 'That wasn't a very cheerful bit of news on Christmas Day.'

'But they'll be suffering much worse.'

I put on the radio to cheer us up. They were playing

Christmas carols. 'Will you listen to the King's Speech at Thomas's?' I asked.

She put away the iron. 'I suppose so. You'll miss it though, won't you?'

'Yes, working until four. Then carols in the billiard room.'

She buttered some toast I'd put on. 'And Grant's supposed to appear today. It's like a mystery. Will he knock on the door any minute, be at work all day, see you in the canteen, or at the carols?'

'And what will he have to say, I wonder. Quick, let's talk about something else while I get ready. This fog is still so thick I'll get the bus again. If I go on my bike, I'll get knocked off sure as sure as God made little green apples.'

Bronwyn reached into a cupboard and pulled out a package. 'Here's your gift. It's not much, Lily, but I hope you like it.'

It was a book, and one I'd wanted for ages. I hugged her, delighted. I went to a different cupboard and took out my gift for her. 'I hope this fits!'

She unwrapped it and gasped. 'It's fabulous, Lil.' She immediately took off her dressing gown and put the jacket on over her pyjamas. She did up the buttons and stroked the fabric as if it were a cat. Then she went into the hall where there was a mirror, turning this way and that admiring herself. 'It fits a treat. You couldn't have given me anything more lush. Gotta say, you're a star!'

We hugged as I headed for the front door, remembering to take a chunk of bread for the dog. 'I hope you have a lovely day with Thomas and Bella,' I said.

* * *

The morning flew by at work and thank goodness I had no correctly spelled code words. The canteen did a half decent midday meal and had some sprigs of holly on each table. I looked around for Grant but he wasn't there, and his wheelchair wasn't outside his office. Deflated, I went back to my desk, wondering if he really would come.

The clock seemed to slow down in the afternoon and each time I looked at it, I became convinced it had stopped. In one of the offices along the corridor they had a radio and turned on the King's Christmas Speech. I couldn't stop to listen to it, but heard the occasional words – 'dark shadow', 'hope', 'thankfulness'. There was a lot to be thankful for, but that didn't take away all the deaths and suffering our poor country had gone through.

At four o'clock sharp, I was relieved of my headset. I tidied my hair and walked through the fog towards the big house. My footsteps on the gravel, which usually sounded sharp and crisp, were muffled as if my feet were yards away from my ears. I'd been back and forward for my breaks, but there was no sign of Grant and I was filled with both hope and confusion. But I could hear 'Away in a Manger' coming from the big house and looked forward to joining in the singing. Then someone I knew from the Beer Hut caught up with me and put her arm through mine. 'Come on, Lily, let's get singing!'

As soon as I saw the billiard room with its beautifully decorated tree, my spirits rose. It might be wartime and dark outside, but there was still plenty to be grateful for. Spending a while singing round the tree with friends was definitely one of those things. I nudged my way into the circle and joined in as a new carol started, 'God Rest You, Merry Gentlemen'. I loved the feeling the singing gave, the exhilaration, the joy of being with like-minded people on this special day.

We had moved on to singing 'Oh, Little Town of Bethlehem'.

'I always said you have a great voice,' someone whispered in my ear.

I smelled him before I saw him.

His favourite cologne, woody and masculine. My breathing got faster and my heart soared.

And there he was.

Grant.

Smiling, reaching out for my hand.

'I have other attributes!' I quipped.

'Oh yes,' he whispered. 'And what might they be?'

I squeezed his hand, never wanting to let it go. 'We'll find out later, shall we?'

He raised my hand to his lips and kissed it, then whispered, 'Forgive me.'

I was so distracted by his presence, by the nearness of him, I was hardly aware of the other carols we sang. Or the others grinning at the sight of our reunion.

When Archie called it a day and suggested we all go to the Beer Hut, I glanced down for the first time and gasped.

Where one of Grant's trouser legs had been pinned up, it was now let down, and he was wearing both shoes. He saw my look and tapped his new leg with his crutch. It gave a metallic ring. 'I'm not used to it yet, this is its first outing. I'll need the wheelchair again before long.'

Ignoring all the people around us, I turned and gave him a massive hug. I never wanted to let him go.

'Do you want to go to the Beer Hut?' he asked. 'My place is warm and I've got some food in, hoping you'll join me.'

I didn't need to think twice about it. 'Let's go straight there,' I said with a cheeky grin.

As we went to the car he'd arranged to take us both back, I looked at him properly. He still had the pain-forged lines on his face that would probably be with him forever, but his colour was healthy and his eyes sparkled. I hadn't seen them like that since before his injury.

The roads were quiet, most people tucked up inside their homes celebrating. In the taxi we huddled close together, his arm round me. I noticed the driver catching sight of us in his rear-view mirror, but I didn't care. Grant put his arms around me, and I cuddled up to him feeling warm and content. All my fears for the future melted away, and I knew I could look forward to my life with this wonderful man. He whispered an apology again, and I put my finger to his lips. 'You never have to apologise. The important thing is you're here now. We're together.'

The driver carried his wheelchair in and said, 'Happy Christmas!' as we paid him. Grant had lit the fire, but it had got lower while he'd been at the Park. I bent down to put some more coal on it as he took his coat off. Using a crutch, he went into the kitchen and returned with a bottle of wine. I looked around the room. He'd tried to make it festive with sprigs of holly and a bunch of twigs decorated with strips of coloured paper. He'd even got some mistletoe hanging from the light.

'You've no idea how hard it was to get this. All thanks to Archie. He's been a good friend, putting up with me and my moods.'

We sat side by side on the sofa, our hips touching, and I felt dizzy with the nearness of him. He poured two glasses of wine, turned to me and held up his glass for a toast.

'To us. To our future together,' he whispered. Then he took a sip of his wine and kissed me tenderly.

'To us.'

Grant bent forward and removed his new artificial leg. The skin was still pink, but the scar looked healthy. 'It rubs a bit, but the hospital say my stump will harden and it will be okay.' He looked at me, concern in his eyes. 'Does seeing it put you off?'

I kissed his cheek. 'When I was with the ARP, I saw much, much worse. You don't need to worry on my account.'

The coal in the fireplace crackled, and I realised I hadn't put the fire guard back. Reluctantly, I let go of his hand and dealt with it.

'Come back here,' he said, his eyes moist. 'I'm so sorry I've been such an idiot. Not seeing you has been the hardest thing I've ever done in my life. I've never felt so low. I couldn't see any future for me at all, with or without you.'

I gulped to hold back a tear. 'I thought you'd never come back to me. I've been so worried.'

He shook his head. 'I should have had more trust in you. I only felt half a man, useless, redundant. I couldn't believe you'd ever want me, no matter how many times you told me it was okay.'

I raised an eyebrow and smiled. 'I'm guessing some other bits of you still work okay.'

He pulled me closer. 'Want to find out?'

I smiled again, glad I'd thought to wear my sexy parachute silk knickers.

POSTSCRIPT

Postcard from Peggy to Lily:

Marion had beautiful boy yesterday. She's calling him David. Small, but doing well. Come and see us! Love Peggy x

POSTSCRIPT.

ABOUT THE AUTHOR

Patricia McBride is the author of several fiction and non-fiction books as well as numerous articles. She loves undertaking the research for her books, helped by stories told to her by her Cockney mother and grandparents who lived in the East End. Patricia lives in Cambridge with her husband.

Sign up to Patricia McBride's mailing list for news, competitions and updates on future books.

Visit Patricia's website: www.patriciamcbrideauthor.com

Follow Patricia on social media here:

facebook.com/patriciamcbrideauthor

instagram.com/tricia.mcbride.writer

ALSO BY PATRICIA MCBRIDE

The Lily Baker Series

The Button Girls

The Picture House Girls

The Telephone Girls

The Air Raid Girls

The Blackout Girls

The Bletchley Park Girls

Christmas Wishes for the Bletchley Park Girls

The Library Girls of the East End Series

The Library Girls of the East End

Hard Times For The East End Library Girls

A Christmas Gift for the East End Library Girls

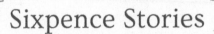

Sixpence Stories

Introducing Sixpence Stories!

Discover page-turning historical novels from your favourite authors, meet new friends and be transported back in time.

Join our book club Facebook group

https://bit.ly/SixpenceGroup

Sign up to our newsletter

https://bit.ly/SixpenceNews

Boldwœd

Boldwood Books is an award-winning fiction publishing company seeking out the best stories from around the world.

Find out more at www.boldwoodbooks.com

Join our reader community for brilliant books, competitions and offers!

Follow us
@BoldwoodBooks
@TheBoldBookClub

Sign up to our weekly deals newsletter

https://bit.ly/BoldwoodBNewsletter

Milton Keynes UK
Ingram Content Group UK Ltd.
UKHW020951210924
1772UKWH00036B/295